The Case of the Captain's Hair

Rhiannon D. Elton

*Dedicated to Marc-Rian Stubbs (1990–2016)
Without you kicking my butt into gear and giving me hope
I would have never reached so far for my dreams and
made them a reality.*

Declaration of Intention

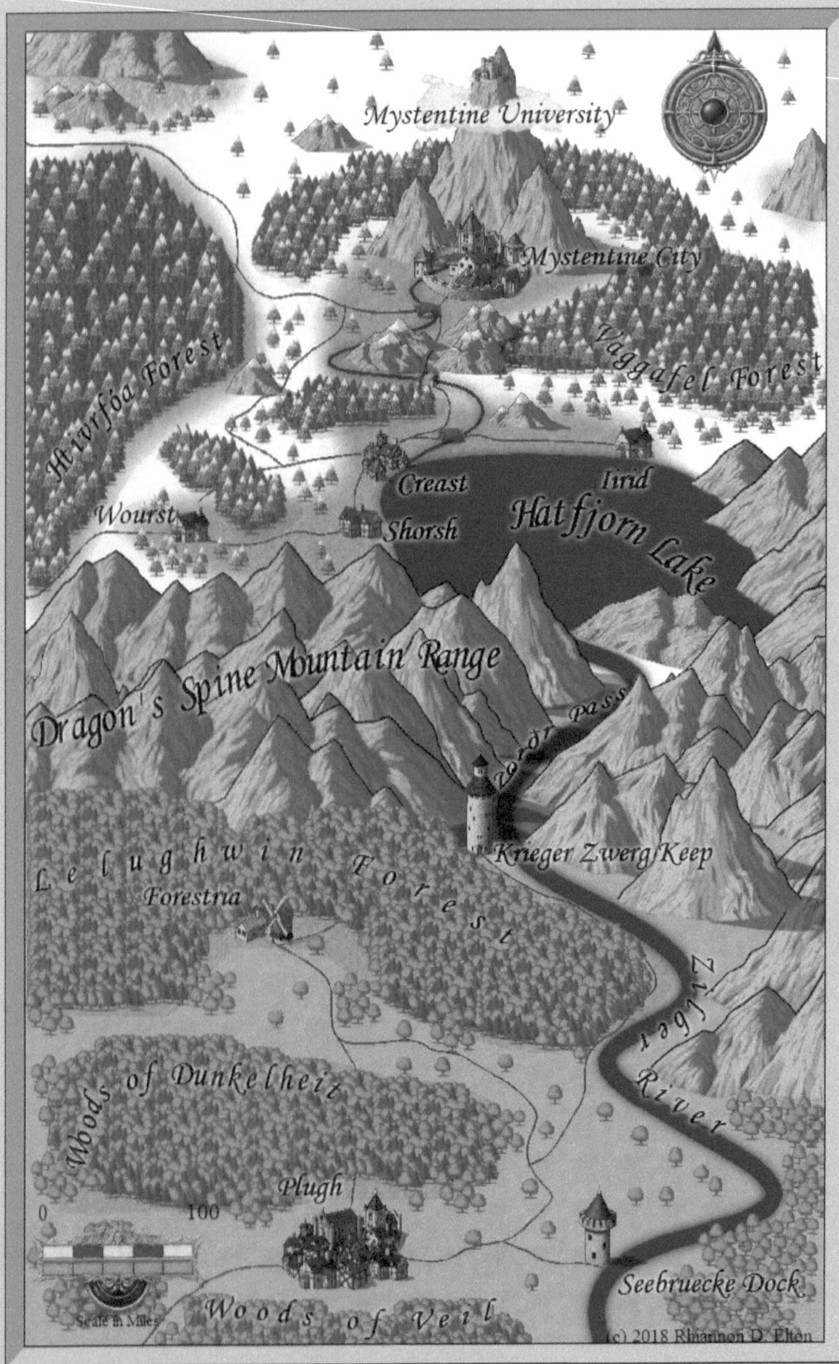

Mystentine University
Mystentine City
Vaggafel Forest
Htivrföa Forest
Wourst
Creast
Shorsh
Tirid
Hatfjorn Lake
Dragon's Spine Mountain Range
Zondr Pass
Lelughwin Forest
Forestria
Krieger Zwerg Keep
Zilbér River
Woods of Dunkelheit
Plugh
0
100
Scale in Miles
Seebruecke Dock
Woods of Veil
(c) 2018 Rhiannon D. Elton

CHAPTER 1
The Felen Family

Dusky orange light glinting through the window signified the end of Wolflock.

No one could drag him to his impending destruction. There was nothing that could make him go.

Surely, he'd be protected by the layers of blanket and curtain from his four-poster bed.

"But you're half dressed. Just put on some shoes and we can go. Ginia is waiting," whined a young girl's disembodied voice.

Wolflock pulled the thick, downy blanket tighter around his head to block out the noise. "She's going to tag along with whatever you do. You don't need my presence."

"I can't hear you through your blanket, brother mine. You just sound like 'mmmfff mfffm, mfffll'," the girl sang back to him before kicking her heels arrhythmically on something wooden.

She's sitting on the dresser. If she kicks any harder on the bottom shelf, she's going to find my-

She stopped kicking as they both heard a loud clinking noise.

"Wolflock? What have you been up to?" she giggled with malicious glee.

"Myna, don't-!"

Wolflock threw off the blankets and tumbled out of his enormous bed as she yanked open his bottom dresser draw. Except for his bedside table, his dresser was the closest item of furniture to his bed, but it was still a good six feet away.

Myna's pudgy little hands had already dug it out.

"Wolflock... really? What is this?"

She rolled her eyes as she pocketed his vial.

"It's none of your business, is what it is." Wolflock stormed across the room and tried to snatch the glass vial from her.

"It is if you're planning on ruining Samhain again." She dodged his grasp and ran to the door leading out to the hallway. "What were you hoping to do, anyway? Make a truth serum?"

She slammed his door shut before he could reach her. He jiggled the door handle, but she held it tight.

"Why would I need a truth serum? They're all horrible liars! Myna, give it back!"

"Get dressed and I'll give it back. It looks like a truth serum. A bit too blue, though. Who did you get to enchant it?"

Wolflock couldn't budge the door, so he punched it and leaned back on it as he slumped to the floor, shaking out the sting on his knuckles before he spoke.

"It isn't meant to be a truth serum. And no one has enchanted it."

"Did *you* try?"

"Of course I didn't."

"Good. It would be fruitless. You can't use magic. You're much too logical, anyway."

"So knowing it's not enchanted, will you give it back?"

"Mmmm... what is it meant to do?"

Wolflock huffed and fidgeted with his uncuffed sleeves. "It's a prototype. I was seeing if I could create an ingested illusion, making it seem as if I was still at the ball even if I wasn't."

Myna fell silent on the other side of the door and,

for a moment, Wolflock thought she had left, having grown bored of the conversation. He opened the door just as his little sister aimed a kick at it, catching his shin instead.

"Ouch!"

She gasped, then scoffed. "Why did you move? I wouldn't have gotten you if you hadn't moved."

"You wouldn't have kicked me, but you would have hit my back with the vibrations from the door." He gripped his shin until the sharp pain melted into a throb.

"I wouldn't have *hit* your back. I would have just pressed it firmly."

Wolflock checked for any blood as he scowled at Myna's antics. Satisfied he was unscathed, he snatched the little bottle back off her and pocketed it. As he retreated towards his bed, he heard his little sister take a quick step to stop him, but, as she didn't catch his hand, he realised she was up to something else.

With a dramatic turn, he flopped back onto his bed, glimpsing Myna leaning up against his door frame with a pensive expression. It couldn't mask the excitement in her acid green eyes, though.

Wolflock's curiosity began to itch in her direction. Nothing could make him go. Of this he was resolute. But what would his persistent sibling try next?

"Fine."

He continued to look at the swirling moulding on the ceiling, knowing it would annoy her more if he didn't respond.

He was right.

She cleared her throat. "Fine."

Wolflock smirked as he pretended not to hear her again.

"I guess I'll just have to try and see what's happening with Miss Thorn's driver myself."

"Who?" He sat up on his elbows and looked at her.

"Oh, you didn't know? Miss Thorn has a new driver. After a bunch of jewellery went missing, he was sent to the guard tower, but she went and fetched him out with a clean record. Strange behaviour for a girl who is meant to be marrying the mayor's son."

Wolflock swung his legs over the bed and pulled on his socks and shoes. "When was he employed?"

Myna's face twitched as she tried to hide a smirk. "Two moons ago, midway through St'lung Luna."

"And when was he put in custody?"

"Just after Mabon. It was said he stole the jewellery while everyone was celebrating."

"Whose jewellery did he steal?"

"Well, that's the funny thing, isn't it?"

Wolflock waited, but Myna just grinned at him with a wicked glint in her eye. After a moment, he sighed, conceding that she had won as he put on his silver bi-cut dodecahedron cufflinks and black suit jacket.

"Those ones? Again?" Myna waddled over to his dresser and dug out his cufflink case.

"I like these ones. The mathematics of geometry is relaxing," He slumped as Myna replaced one of his silver ones with a sapphire set.

"I got these for you for Yule and I'm yet to see you wear them."

"It would annoy you to no end if I went out with one sapphire one and my geometric one."

He let her finish dressing him as she saw fit, knowing while she focused on making him presentable, she would answer his questions.

"So, whose jewels were stolen?"

"Miss Thorn's jewels."

She would have hated that, Wolflock thought as smug satisfaction bubbled in him. *She values her trinkets more than people.*

"Who reported the theft?"

"One of Miss Thorn's friends, Miss Gerschwin."

"The one with the pug face who shines her hair

with fish oil?"

"Apparently, it's meant to improve mental acuity," Myna replied in her usual manner of agreeing without causing offence.

As Myna spoke, a long, deep groan trembled through the room. Both siblings froze as it occurred and looked about, hunting for the source, but it came from all around.

"See? Even the house thinks Miss Gerschwin is a boring subject. It's yawning," Wolflock snorted, breaking the eerie silence.

"No. It's yawning because it thought it could get a good night's sleep and we're leaving after its bedtime. Regardless, the pug faced fish oiled one is indeed Miss Gerschwin."

"I thought she and Miss Thorn had a falling out over her engagement to the mayor's son."

"You are most certainly correct. There was a rather public clash where Miss Gerschwin toppled the maypole at Beltaine when she found out. They've since become acquaintances again."

Wolflock made a face as Myna tugged a comb through his pitch-black hair. *Knowing Miss Thorn, she likely believes she can still get something out of Miss Gerschwin. What does the driver have to do with it, though? Is Miss Thorn using him to spy on other ladies? Or is he a thief of his own accord? And if so, why would she pay such kindness to a man she could easily replace? If she is using him as a spy, that would explain why she rescued him after he allegedly stole her property. It would also give her entire family the means of spying on the other courtiers in Plugh...*

"There. Dashing. Let's collect father and we'll be on our way," Myna chimed in, breaking Wolflock from his thoughts.

She linked her arm through his and led him down the hallway to their father's study, dodging the staff carrying decorations down the hall. It was normal for Myna to drag both Wolflock and their father around when she had a goal. She often forgot they were still attached if she became entranced by her objectives.

A trait that, admittedly, ran in the family.

Darkness and stagnation met them as they approached his office. The heavy, faded red curtains were perpetually drawn in their father's wing, and very few of the staff were permitted in his quarters. It was no mystery to anyone what he was trying to hide or why he guarded his secrets so possessively. With children like Myna and Wolflock, nothing stayed private for long.

Before Myna could raise her right hand to knock

on the dark oak door, the house around them groaned and sighed again. Both siblings froze and Myna gripped Wolflock's arm with both hands.

"You do it."

"He's not that frightening." Wolflock rolled his eyes.

"The house said you should be the one to do it."

"It's just yawning again. It's hardly an omen."

"Don't you hear it at night? I swear it's ghosts or something."

Wolflock made a face and rapped his knuckles on the door. "You know better than to talk about ghosts around father. He's already prone to bouts of melancholy around Samhain."

They waited a few moments before the sound of a heavy chair moving across old carpet emanated from the other side of the door. They pressed their ears to the wood and heard draws shut, locks clicked, and papers shuffled.

The pair of them mouthed a silent argument about what he was doing. Wolflock mimed his father putting away contracts behind his safe hidden behind the painting of their great grandparents, while Myna mimicked the motions of stashing a bag in a secret compartment in his desk drawers. The door dropped away from their ears and they both jumped back, staring up at the towering figure that was their father.

Falcon Felen stood broad and tall with ebony hair, streaked with silver, and the same acid green eyes as his daughter. The three of them bore a chilling stare even when they didn't mean to, but, in this moment, Mr Felen senior definitely intended to fix it on them.

"Is it time?" thrummed his baritone voice. No matter how much he smoked his pipe, the history of music could not be forgotten in his vocal prowess.

"Yes, Father. I believe Gruta is waiting for us at the carriage. If my calculations are correct, she will remember she has forgotten my clutch and retrieve it by the time we make it down." Myna tapped her chin as she thought.

Wolflock rolled his eyes. He should have known Myna would have orchestrated some manipulation with precision when she hadn't tussled with him. She resorted to physical manipulation only when she was out of ideas. He should have waited longer and he may not have been made to go.

At least now he'd be able to dig up more dirt on Aiirika Thorn and find out what power she had over her driver. More importantly, he'd be able to uncover what she was plotting next.

The challenge would make the evening less of a waste.

Something not quite tucked into his father's trouser pocket caught his eye. A silk cloth shimmered in the dwindling lantern light. A lady's handkerchief? Or a small shawl? Wolflock glimpsed passed his father and saw his enormous, dark oak desk. As he expected, the picture of his smiling mother framed in intricate gold glinted back at him.

His face scrunched with uncomfortable feelings. Every Samhain his father brought that same picture out, as if she would magically materialise in front of it.

Rhiannon D. Elton

CHAPTER 2
The Best in Plughian Society

Myna took her father's huge hand in her tiny one and led both men down the stairs. Wolflock slouched behind them as far as Myna's grasp would let him. Even with the allure of a puzzle to solve over the course of the evening, he didn't want to go. He would just allow himself to be dragged to a slightly less terrible doom.

The three Felen's descended the sweeping staircase to the entrance hall in time to see Gruta, their governess race down the stairs with a shiny satin orange clutch and black beading to match Myna's dress.

"Oh! Miss Myna! There you are. Your bag. I did have to clean out the old candies, though. What if you had gotten them stuck to your dance mates? You'll have plenty of sweets when you get home."

Gruta was younger than she looked, but caring for the Felen children over the past decade had aged her significantly. Her face was creased easily with every expression she made, and her chestnut hair rippled with black and grey strands, but she remained otherwise in sturdy health. Mr Felen Senior took careful care of all those in his employ.

The towering gentleman aided the ladies down the front stone stairs and into the elegant mahogany carriage trimmed with gold filigree and sporting a scarlet velvet interior. The driver, Huston, sat ready to take off with two of their black mares.

Wolflock frowned before he entered the carriage and took his seat by Myna.

"Where is Brennan?"

Mr Felen Senior took his seat inside the carriage and stood his horse-headed cane against the wall.

"It's Samhain, brother mine. Brennan's hardly the right look for Samhain." Myna smoothed her dress on her lap.

She had been a bit too smug for Wolflock's liking. He'd have to find a way to annoy her to get back at her and to show her who was the oldest.

"His spots look very mask-like, and his white is

ghostly, but it was requested that you didn't spend all night talking to him and avoiding the festivities," Gruta sighed, perceiving the oncoming confrontation. "If you do well this year I'm sure we can talk about Brennan leading the carriage into town next year."

Wolflock scowled. He was certain Myna had a hand in this, too.

He felt her little acid green eyes boring into him, begging for him to rile up. She was humming with excitement and didn't know where to direct it. Instead of giving her the pleasure of an argument, Wolflock decided to let her stew. Gruta started a conversation about who would be attending and the opportunities for education, career and investments, but Wolflock took that as his queue to be free of the idle prattle.

He rested his elbow on the thin windowsill and rested his chin in his spindly hand, staring out at the places they passed. Many of the common grounds were places he actively avoided. Not for any snobbery or classist position, but more for the fact that he hated having to talk with people about anything less than the highest intellectual pursuits. He wished more people could open conversations about which chemical formulas could be used for revealing fingerprints most accurately, or what different shoe materials looked like on various flooring.

The only commons he liked were the libraries, and even those were limited.

Wolflock had avoided many unwanted social interactions by reading every book in the common library and in their private one. Myna often said to him that he would have far more reading material if he made friends. It's not like he didn't try. His attempts at civility and creating bonds were quickly rebuked once newcomers became acquainted with the poor history he had with the longstanding nobility. And common folk were never educated in any capacity he found remotely interesting.

Their carriage clacked passed the little parks scattered through Plugh like ink flicked from a stiff paintbrush. All manner of people had gathered through the macabrely decorated streets. The colours of Samhain were all things brown, orange, yellow, red and black. Pumpkins cut with wicked faces winked with candlelight on every terrace. Paper lanterns lit by the pixies that flitted from one to the other dangled from the trees overhanging the main roads. Haunting vibrato from stringed instruments warbled around every corner. Paper skeletons and skulls hung behind windows, and the dog-sized mechanical spider out the front of *Snickelgrubers Music Box Click Clacks* moved its delicately cogged front four legs, spooking passing children.

Gasps, cheers and laughter splashed against the window as people in masks pulled their pranks and made their merry. Tables adorned with cheap black tablecloths overflowed with the last major harvest of the year, available for anyone in Plugh to take and do with what they wanted for the Winter.

Witches zoomed past them on their broomsticks, flitting like the pixies from one house to another, offering protection, wards, charms and blessings. Wolflock didn't want to talk to any of these people, but he could see their genuine smiles and wished he could just observe the middle city for the night instead of going to the Samhain Ball.

They passed his favourite alchemist, Aquilla Tofana, outside of her shop *Shell Potions and Stores*, who gave him his old textbooks. Soon after they rode passed the baker, Borris Dracodor, who always gave him and extra apple scroll for Brennan, the tailor, Sinch Wincher, who would stitch in an extra pocket his father and Gruta wouldn't know about, and the scribe, Jyne Twain, who would let him read the old books if he could translate them into the local language. As long as he was left alone, he could entertain himself happily.

He visited these places infrequently, but, while they were here, Plugh held at least some happiness for him. Without them, this city would be nothing more than a nightmare.

Wolflock felt better, having successfully avoided conversation until the carriage pulled to a halt at the valet station. They had reached the centre of Plugh, the royal palace and seat of all things Wolflock despised.

They weren't the only attendees running late, as the valet station was filled with the shiniest, most elegant carriages the crafts folk in Plugh had designed. All those with positions remotely close to the crown came from far and wide to attend the Sabbat parties held by the royal family of Grothener. Knowing that the various fae courts may also attend was a big part of the excitement. Getting into the good graces of a fae could mean extravagant prosperity for the season ahead, which would create a cascade of good fortune for those around them and the country itself.

Wolflock did not care.

Myna was as close to a fairy as he hoped to be, and she didn't have a trace of fae heritage.

He stepped out of the carriage first, greeted by a juggler tossing flaming daggers and an acrobat tumbling through them in the air. Ladies of the Autumn fae court flew in place high above them with slow beating monarch butterfly wings, showering the attendees in white, red and yellow petals. Young children wore little suits, ballgowns and full-face masks of all kinds: he could see butterfly wings, bow truckles, gnomes, and porcelain dolls. Masks all to deceive the spirits that came out on Samhain to cause mischief and mayhem.

"Wolflock! You don't have your mask," Myna whined as their father helped her down. Sometime towards the end of the carriage ride she had adorned herself with a smirking pumpkin mask made of plaster and painted orange. It would have looked very peasant-like if not for the black lace frilling around and over it.

"No one here needs one. Their faces suffice," Wolflock scoffed, crossing his arms as he looked around for the Thorn's driver.

"I knew he would say that," Gruta said as she stepped down with Mr Felen's help. "So, I brought this." She passed him a very simple white mask with cat's eye points at the edges. "Don't get into any trouble this early in the night, please. I would like one pumpkin pie before I have to escort you home."

Wolflock scowled.

Without a word, Mr Felen led Gruta inside and Myna expectantly held out her arm for Wolflock to take, pouting when he stepped off without her. His piercing blue eyes glanced to the sides, noting the carriages, and to the palace windows, seeing if anyone he recognised lurked in the hallways outside the ballroom. His mind fired into action like dormant embers in a forge, each new piece of data blowing the bellows as he forged intricate new threads of his metallic mental web.

The carriage nearest to them was the newest. An open topped, sleek black phaeton with the Grothien symbols for R.H. embossed in gold on the back. Even without the initials, Wolflock knew who it belonged to. Such an impractical, pretty thing could only belong to the Mayor of Plugh's son, Rechen von Herren. Wolflock hadn't seen this particular model racing about town yet, so he believed it to not only be new, but also imported. The wheel had already been scuffed from Rechen's terrible driving, and, judging by the circumference and colour of the scratches, he had hit two gutters on Parkvay Drive and Bakers Lane. From the strong waft of perfume emanating from the carriage, Wolflock could ascertain that Rechen had picked up multiple passengers in order to show off his new carriage. He would have driven recklessly in order to show his acquaintances what the vehicle was capable of, but, as he was a poor driver at the best of times with an excessive amount of confidence in his limited capabilities, the scratches were imminent.

Guessing from the oaky cologne smells, his

passengers were likely to be two of the other young men he often fooled around with.

Wise to not bring a lady in his fast new carriage tonight. Miss Thorn wouldn't take the slight lightly. Wolflock thought as he looked over the next few carriages, identifying who was attending the ball and who they had come with.

The Worwest family had come in their old wagon and, from the smell of fresh polish yet the shine not reaching the less obvious areas, he could see that they were still in financial turmoil. They had no driver, so it must have been quite dire as Mr Worwest senior would have driven the family. The shame of having to drive himself and the old nag of a horse through the city to the palace meant that he hoped to change his fortunes. As the beast looked exhausted, Wolflock ascertained that the entire family would be present.

He's lining up an advantageous match for his eldest, Nahten. It won't work though. Nahten is one of the weakest willed, indecisive boys I've ever met. He tries to have a fling with any lady who is present before flopping to the next with every rebuke. Gahten would be a far better option. Quiet and taciturn, he would at least take the affair seriously. I wonder if Nahten's friendship with the Thorn boys is what allowed this potential match this evening...

Beside them was a stagecoach with a well-kept body and all new wheels.

Of course the Augrubers would get new wheels before the ball. They'd have to explain why Furon had decided to take an axe to them. You can see where they painted over the gashes marking the sides of the carriage. Lady Augruber must have had these made fresh this week.

The youngest son of the Augruber family was known for his unsavoury temper and bouts of sudden violence against anything he couldn't hold still. Wheels were a complex object that seemed to irritate his dull mind. Wolflock remembered the time he had made a pulley system with belts and a thimble so he could have the library book pages turned while he took notes and sketched from them. After a satisfying day learning about the physics of animal movement he had left the library with his contraption and had the misfortune of meeting Furon before he could get to the carriage. The larger boy had spun the wheels on his page turner so hard a belt snapped and the whole device fell apart onto the ground. The spinning wheels sent Furon into a fit and he stomped them all to bent pieces of rubble before running off laughing.

It was until that time that Wolflock had felt himself a good acquaintance with Euron, Furon's older brother, but, when Euron defended his brother's actions without remorse, Wolflock had ended the acquaintance in anger.

Another family present included the Slarv boys and their elderly grandmother, sent up from the South of Grothener to avoid scandal. Although, they always seemed to be on the boundaries of new ones in Plugh. Their stylish, outdated carriage stood worn but well looked after. Their driver would be inside assisting their grandmother. She was a stubborn old woman who only allowed her driver to act as her servant. She had no other staff for herself even though her grandsons insisted on having others employed under them. Wolflock often suspected that she intended on using her manservant, Erald, as blackmail to keep the young boys in line. The threat of giving him everything and the boys nothing in her will was something everyone had claimed to hear, yet never had evidence of.

One of the more modern carriages amongst the lines was the Truls'. Father and son, Paretti Senior and Junior had roots in Shellinden, where political ambition and studies of the arts sat at the feet of the Emperor. Paretti senior had come to Plugh as a young man and wove himself into the circus of the court, quickly becoming the ringleader for the clowns who thought themselves above all others. He told stories about how he was instrumental in the late Empress Revari's success and training her daughters, but Wolflock didn't believe a word of it.

Without evidence of any kind, it was all hearsay, but he'd also heard Paretti Senior talk about meeting with the King of Grothener at the same time their King had been travelling throughout the East to meet with dignitaries from other nations. His lies had convinced the other courtiers and helped put his son in valuable investment positions, but Wolflock remained distrustful.

He couldn't imagine the imperial family would associate with charlatans like that. They had far too much important business to conduct. The Emperor was also the King of Shellinden and Shiriling, as were all of his ancestors going back at least a thousand years. Being tutored by conniving fiends like Paretti Truls the elder was beneath them.

As expected, next to the Truls' carriage stood the most gaudy, impractical show of wealth anyone had ever seen. It hurt Wolflock's eyes to even look at it.

It's as if they think they're royalty... he scoffed as he eyed the gigantic coach, fitted with swirling waves of gold filigree that clutched rubies like holly berries. The afternoon light glinted and winked off the polished waves, casting shadows that made even the softest curves on the carriage look edged like knives.

The Thorn's carriage dominated the space even more than the five-tiered fountain beside it. From Wolflock's position, it looked like the carriage was the fountain and the water was spraying from the top of it.

He stepped closer, keeping an eye for anyone but Myna watching him, and peeked at the driver's platform. Their driver was the regular one. A thin man who smoked stinking herbs from a cheap little pipe. His uniform was a little too short for him and he shuffled his pants and suspenders several times as he hadn't adjusted the straps correctly. He looked as welcoming as a starving street dog.

That can't be the one Myna was talking about...

Wolflock frowned, glancing around the carriage. A diminutive version of the gaudy beast nestled beside it. The second carriage was part of a matching set and the fresh flowers arranged over the back of the carriage told Wolflock this was the one he had been looking for.

Miss Thorn came separately. But why? Is she plotting something she doesn't want her father to be aware of?

A thin stream of smoke came from the front of the

smaller carriage and Wolflock could hear the turn of a page.

That doesn't sound like a newspaper. Has Miss Thorn found a driver who can read?

Before Myna could stop him, he walked to see the front of the carriage and who was so important to Miss Thorn's evil schemes that she would bail out a common servant.

His piercing blue eyes were met with impenetrable pastel green, as if he had expected to see someone come around to where he was reading. The driver watched Wolflock without fear or trepidation, with intelligent eyes and a cocky smirk. Thick brown hair poked out of the rim of his cap and he lounged across the seat as if it were his private room. In his hands he held a well-worn library book that Wolflock glimpsed as an old, religious text for the goddess of fortune, Verulle.

"Merry meet, Felen." The young driver had a sarcastic voice tinged with a chuckle that sounded like wood crinkling in a fireplace. Wolflock didn't like how he addressed him so informally.

"You know me, sir?"

"Sure. Yeah. Let's call it that." The driver shrugged and slid down between Wolflock and the carriage.

Drivers weren't normally this disrespectful or sly.

It unnerved the young sleuth.

"I saw smoke and wanted to make sure no one was damaging Miss Thorn's carriage," he lied.

The driver, who stood a little taller than Wolflock, leaned his arm on the foot stand and jerked his head to the little glass ashtray on the seat. "She's trying to get me to quit."

"I see it's working well, then. As persuasive as always."

Something dangerous flashed in the driver's eyes. "The carriage is fine."

Wolflock shrugged. He'd hit the end of the man's patience, so he may as well try a harder approach. "Is it true Miss Thorn paid for your release after stealing from her? Very generous of her if it is true."

"Yeah? So what if it is?"

"Well, it's not like Miss Thorn to keep a servant around. I'm sure she barely knows the names of any of them. The Thorn family staff come and go like birds to a garden. It's just a point of curiosity, really. Why would she put her neck and purse out for you after you'd stolen from her? Does she have you indentured now?"

The sardonic laugh that met his ears was not what Wolflock expected.

"She talked you up, you know? In her own way.

Told me to keep an eye out for you. Told me you were always problematic and meddling. I don't know why. Listen. I saw you eyeing off all the carts here. I ain't stealing nothing and I definitely ain't letting you snoop around her wheels. Go poke your nose in at the ball and stir trouble there. I'll look forward to hearing all about it on the drive home."

Wolflock's eyes narrowed. The driver was Miss Thorn's spy. Several mentions of her speaking directly to him, telling him things, listening to gossip, the confidence of his position, the forewarning of Wolflock looking around. But there was something more.

Mentioning that Miss Thorn was 'trying to get him to quit' smoking, 'in her own way', and his brief glare when Wolflock insulted her. Was Miss Thorn close to this staff member? Or was his apparent affection single sided?

"Wolflock!" Myna hissed and pulled his arm. "Stop being a nuisance! Father is waiting."

As he allowed Myna to drag him away, he looked back at the strange driver, who winked and flicked his fingers under his hat in a sarcastic 'Merry part' motion. Little green sparks of magic trailed after his fingertips as Myna hauled Wolflock into the entrance hall.

"Where was he?" Gruta sighed with relief as they

approached.

"Observing the Thorn's new matching carriages," his sister answered.

Their father remained stoic, looking at his intricate silver pocketwatch. The siblings exchanged glances, knowing that was the warning sign of them nearly running late.

The pretty sound of the string quartet on the mezzanine above them couldn't mask the uncomfortable silence that befell the room. They hadn't even been announced. Ladies in Samhain shaded ball gowns snapped their fans open to whisper gossip behind them and gentlemen quaffed, turning their backs just enough to pretend they hadn't seen them.

Wolflock set his jaw and glanced to the rest of his party to see if they would acknowledge the unfriendly reception. Gruta began stammering nervously about how she needed a cool drink and how warm the room was. His father stared at every person intensely until they acknowledged him with a nod, to which he returned the sentiment. Myna's bottom eyelids lifted just a touch, as if she were a stalking cat hunting for any twittering birds, too stupid to be vocal within earshot.

At least I'm not the only one on edge. Not that it will do us any good.

"Do you think they're still mad about the Beltaine ball?" Gruta swallowed.

Myna snickered and Wolflock rolled his eyes. "No. That was last year. I'm sure this year it's about the Lammas prizes." he drawled.

"Didn't you fix that?" Gruta whispered.

"It's not the Lammas prizes." Myna continued to snicker. She always got the giggles when she knew something Wolflock and her father weren't aware of. "The current attitude is from Wolflock's run in with the Autumn fae stealing the Ostara eggs."

"Didn't you fix that too?" Gruta's worry lines deepened.

"I did. Evidently helping the city appease the Spring fae who were meant to be there has left a few people complicit in the matter disgruntled." Wolflock brushed down his sleeve.

"Well, it's the Autumn fae who are guests tonight, so-" Gruta struggled to come up with some instruction she thought he would take.

"Avoid them," Falcon Felen's deep voice thrummed softly as he eyed his son. That was the last say in the matter.

Attendants offered them bubbling apple juice and roasted chestnuts on little fig cakes. Wolflock declined, but the others accepted the offer, beginning to relax.

Myna ate four of the little cakes quickly and wiped her mouth. "Mayor von Herren will be in the sitting room by the ballroom. She'll likely have one dance every hour in order to keep Master Rechen in line. The Thorn's will be in the same place, but Miss Thorn will skim between there and the garden once dinner is finished. I'm off to find Ginia. Find me if you need anything else."

Wolflock and his father blinked at one another as Myna waved them off and trotted away. Gruta bit her lip, glancing from Wolflock to Myna, nervous to leave either of them alone.

"I suppose you'd best stay with me as I'm prone to far more trouble than Myna," he sneered at his governess.

Gruta narrowed her brown eyes, then took a few steps towards the rapidly departing Myna. After a few more moments she made up her mind and took off after the youngest child, leaving Wolflock smug.

"Myna is correct in saying you plan on harassing the Thorn's this evening?" Mr Felen senior hummed.

"Only as far as spoiling any nefarious schemes they may be embroiling."

"Very well. I have business with Mayor von Herren."

The implication was for Wolflock to join his father in the ballroom adjacent to the sitting room. He and his father often only needed two sentences of dialogue to achieve a full conversation. Everything was up front, to the point, and could be clearly extrapolated. Myna on the other hand required all her words to be teased and translated as she very rarely could be pinned down to a single meaning.

They walked down the hallway to the left towards the first sitting room. Exquisite artworks of all the ancient monarchs and highest nobles lined the hall between towering windows to the left and sophisticated furnishings to the right. Couples, friends and acquaintances sat on the elegant furnishings, but those waiting for the rest of their party hung by the windows, while servants brought canapes. Wolflock knew most of them and, although they had a small place in his mental web, they were insignificant.

The uniformed attendants by the high doors opened it as Mr Felen and Wolflock approached, allowing them access to the sitting room. The deep red room had one wall lined with books from floor to ceiling, with several tables and sofas positioned about to create five little clusters on which people could convene. Mayor von Herren stood by the fireplace laughing with Firenz

Thorn, the uncle of Aiirika Thorn.

Firenz was the most likeable out of all the Thorns, but that said very little. The Mayor wore a shimmering cream dress with a crimson shoulder sash bearing the symbols of the Imperial moon dragon, the Grothien royal family stag, and the mayoral badger.

"Merry meet, Mayor von Herren," Mr Felen interjected in the conversation. "And happy birthday, of course. Apologies for the interruption Firenz. May I have a quick word alone?"

Firenz blinked at the abruptness coming so soon after his joke. "Uh, yes. Of course, Falcon. Come have a drink with us later. I promised Aiirika I'd dance with her friends, but I'll need a substitute. My feet aren't what they used to be."

He chortled away, oblivious to the lack of response Mr Felen returned.

"Merry meet, Falcon. You look excited this evening. How can I be of service?"

Wolflock couldn't tell if the mayor was joking or not, but, as his father started to speak, he glanced about the room. It stank of potpourri, woodsmoke and whatever the quaffing dignitaries were drinking; something like one of those foul wines made from perfectly good grapes or last harvest fruit. Wolflock had been given a glass last Samhain and barely had a sip before he had decided that a nearby pot plant would like it more.

This was the room of eligible bachelors and the debutantes' parents and grandparents. Older suits, more modest dresses, and an air of confidence in their position in society slaked the atmosphere. The heavy drawn curtain left the room stuffy but offered the privacy the adult elite echelon required.

When the royal family held a Sabbat party, they invited all dignitaries, business owners, and landowners. Sometimes hopeful investors, disgruntled staff or lovesick fanatics would try to gain entry. Normally the guardsmen could tell who was trouble or who was out of place, but, in order to avoid having noses pressed up against windows, the sitting room curtains remained drawn.

The only source of vibrant light came from the tall door leading into the ballroom. The music funnelled into the sitting room and curiosity drew Wolflock to the opening. The high glass ceiling arched over the room with a spider web of bronze beams raising golden chandeliers above the polished amber floor and the dancers that twirled like falling leaves.

The room was lined with chairs and tables for weary dancers to rest, and with the Autumn Court fae present, no one was left without a dance partner. Which was exactly why Wolflock hung back in the room. Dancing could be an elegant diversion, but he was intent on finding Miss Thorn. No doubt, if he managed to engage in their usual uncivil conversation, would she inadvertently reveal the secrets she had primed her driver to collect for her. From that information, Wolflock would be able to ascertain what her plot for the next season would be and how he could interrupt it.

Many of the less intelligent courtiers believed this was a game between them, but Wolflock knew it was far more than that. Stopping the Thorn family's nefarious schemes were crucial to the best interests of Plugh and, possibly, all of Grothener.

He watched the orchestra playing on a giant golden pumpkin in the middle of the ballroom, with a spiral of sparkling golden stairs spiralling from the floor to the top platform. His favourite instrument, the mystical *voce'angelii* was not among them and, as they played the usual Samhain list, he grew bored. Wolflock wished more musicians would experiment with their music, but, unfortunately, it provided an easy living to pander to the lowest common requests.

Standing along the back wall, surrounded by his throng of admirers and ladder climbers, Rechen von

Herren waved his hand, telling elaborate stories to the delight of those around him. Among them were Nahten and Gahten, the Worwest boys. That meant that the Thorn's gang would be nearby.

Wolflock glanced back to his father, now in animated conversation with the mayor and the silk shawl clutched between them.

"Once Rechen's wedding is done on Ostara, we will be able to hire some of the wizards from Mystentine and we'll locate her. It's the least we can do after all you've done for the city, Falcon. Besides, when the family resources between the von Herrens and the Thorns are combined, I'm sure I'll be able to do much more to help the town. We may even be able to convert your old country house into something." Mayor von Herren smiled warmly at Mr Felen.

Confident his father was too engrossed in conversation to stop him, he slunk along the edge of the ballroom, avoiding any of the Autumn fae eyes, lest they accost him for a very high dance.

CHAPTER 3
Ballroom Blunders

He circled around the room and spotted the Thorn brothers, Keinz and Eiken, and the Slarv twins by the glass doors leading out to the garden. Keinz put his arm around his brother, moving a letter out of his breast pocket by accident. He snatched it back up before anyone could notice, but Wolflock saw a distinct lip print in a unique shade of plum lip stain.

Are they standing guard for something their little sister is up to? Wolflock wondered as he reached the side table next to Rechen's audience. Two of the boys among them had the distinct oaky cologne Wolflock had noticed outside, and one of them had a smear of brown lipstick along his collar. A similar lipstick was on the wrist of a lady who resembled a borzoi hound with her silky straight hair dropping like pins over her brown chiffon dress.

Nahten stood at the back, leaning into a young, tanned lady's personal space as he loudly whispered, "...And of course you're aware that my position in society would be supremely advantageous to anyone in the merchant field. And, unlike my other friend, I would pursue a woman versed in commerce far more honourably than my friend..."

The girl looked uncomfortable as he spoke, desperate to escape to more amicable company. She pointed to the Thorns and Slarvs as they beckoned Nahten to join them. A new gold necklace on Varush Slarv caught Wolflock's eye. It had intricate beads, but he couldn't tell at a distance what was written on them. It looked familiar, though. From his recollection, Keinz had owned that necklace in the past. His brother, Venuck, seemed to be wearing quite a bit of face powder this evening, but his full glasses of drink revealed an odd plum coloured stain around his mouth.

All of them laughed and clapped on queue for every whim Rechen had. Their smiles looked hungry for the prestige, wealth and power Rechen's position in society held and they grasped to him to desperately remain by his side as he continued his ascension.

Wolflock sneered at their pitiful pretentions. There was one face on the peripheries of the gaggle that caught his eye, though. Etched with a smile that looked more like a snarl, Paretti Truls junior clapped and laughed with the crowd, but his pristine white teeth remained a touch too bared when he smiled.

Wolflock knew more about Paretti senior than his son, but he'd had no quarrel with the young socialite. Why would he have such animosity towards Rechen? Are they not cut from the same cloth? They are very similar in temperament, fashion and purpose. Perhaps too similar.

Paretti caught his eye and his smile dropped immediately. He made unblinking eye contact with Wolflock before snapping.

"What?"

Wolflock just rolled his eyes and turned, heading towards the doors to the courtyard. He could feel Paretti's glare burning into his back, but the young toff couldn't do anything to distress him. The Thorn brothers were a different story, though.

Although they were only a few years older than Wolflock, they stood over six feet tall with frames like bulls. Huge, boorish, and hulking, they were a key reason no one ever picked a fight with Miss Thorn. More than once Wolflock had found himself chased through the back streets of Plugh all the way home by the great lummoxes. Sometimes for riling up their sister with sarcasm or intervening in her plans, and sometimes just because she was bored and would set them on him.

At a royal Sabbat ball, though, he assumed they would be on their best behaviour. Regardless, he'd rather not have the braincell they shared be fired up at the sight of him. Aiming his step to be in time with passing Autumn fae, he stayed out of view, then ducked to the doors with his back to them.

Thankfully, the Thorn brothers and their doltish friends were too engrossed in a conversation about a new carriage manufacturer. Wolflock successfully slipped from the ballroom and into the dewy evening air. Couples strode about the old gardens, screened by hedges, rose bushes, old willows and the columns holding up the terraces that were covered in ancient wisteria vines.

The fresh air cleared Wolflock's mind and he prowled through the garden with a single focus. He had to find Miss Thorn and either spy on her conversation for something to be revealed, or, his more usual method when interacting with her; verbally pummel her until she became so angry she'd let something slip.

He made his way past several couples he knew

weren't publicly courting, trying to hide their enthusiasm for the company they kept when they noticed him. He even found Myna and her red haired friend Ginia in deep conversation about possible infrastructure changes to the town and how they would impact Ginia's father's bakery. Just as he was about to resign himself to searching the palace interior instead, he heard a familiar cackle from inside the hedge maze on the border of the courtyard.

Creeping as lightly as he could, Wolflock entered the browning maze, keeping his right hand grazing the leaves to keep on track. After just two turns he caught a glimpse of the rotund Miss Thorn and smelt the pungent cigarette smoke from her driver.

They laughed together for a moment before silence fell.

"Are you going to tell me what these are now? Or do I have to keep guessing?" her driver chuckled.

"Oh, go on. Give me one more guess and then I'll tell you."

Wolflock felt bile in the back of his throat as she laid on a sickly sweet tone.

"Are these the forgeries you had your last man take, and now you have to return them, otherwise you won't be able to get married and rule the city?"

She cackled again like a goat. "Why do you have

such excellent ideas? No, no. Fine. I'll tell you. These are father's new proposals for factories to be placed in the foothills North of the city. There's one for a huge mill that also takes care of baking, a cotton farm and factory to make clothes at a scale you've never seen, and a potion brewer that also creates beer and wine. My favourite one is for a new concept I came up with called a scribe press. You'll like that one most. It makes books without needing a scribe, all identical and in huge amounts. I can print all your textbooks for your studies that way."

"Ah, and, like the high wizard Margon of old, you will be my king and tell me all you need me to learn."

"And you shall inevitably betray me to the wolves and rebels. At least I'll never be forgotten, but no one shall speak my name. Now, get back to the carriage before anyone notices you're gone. The last thing I need is for Felen to start snooping around. Are you sure you didn't give him any hints?"

Her driver put his hand on her waist a little too fondly. "He's not as smart as he thinks he is. Now, you have fun. Cause Miss Gerschwin trouble for me. I want to hear everything when you're finished."

"I'll drop these on her desk. That way, it will look like the whole town is demanding them and not just us. Then I'll find a reason to leave early."

Wolflock had heard enough. He moved away before they parted. The wretched girl was on the cusp of destroying the last few things he liked about this forsaken town. Miss Thorn had been playing the long game. For months she had been engaged to the Mayor's son purely for this purpose. Plans like this would take at least a season to develop. What she was proposing would ruin all the artisan careers for those industries and then the Thorn's would own the monopoly. Just like they always aimed to do.

His favourite alchemist, baker, tailor, scribe... all of them would be completely out of business, unable to compete with the Thorn's cheap labour and cheap products. That, as well as the Thorns always cutting corners with their productions; the natural world around them decayed, their workers were never safe, and their new products never lasted. It took an enormous scandal and a kidnapped child for their cheap chipboard furniture factory to be shut down, but, by that time, they had forced the local carpenters to sell their tools and many couldn't reopen.

The hospital couldn't afford the subpar medical equipment during a time of crisis when they had taken over the board of directors. Everything they touched, they sapped of all goodness and sustainability until it was destroyed. He couldn't let that happen. Not this time. Not to the few good people left in this town.

Wolflock threw open the doors to the ballroom and charged across the dancefloor, ignoring the jeers from the Thorn brothers. He ducked under the embrace of an autumn fae trying to bring him into the jaunty dance the orchestra had struck up and flew towards the sitting room. As he neared the door, his father and Mayor von Herren emerged, smiling and preparing to join the dancing.

"Father!" Wolflock panted. "Father, I have to speak to you."

Mr Felen's smile faded. "What is the matter?"

"I just heard... Miss Thorn... She has plans that will.... Destroy industries in the town!"

"Head on for a moment, Mayor von Herren. I'll be there in a moment." Mr Felen patted her arm and released it.

The mayor gave Wolflock a nod and stepped towards the drinks table.

"Wolflock, what-"

"She said she's going to create factories that will endanger all the bakers, scribes, alchemists and-"

"Whatever you heard, I order you to drop it."

Wolflock felt like he'd been slapped with a cold

rag. "What?"

"Let this Aiirika Thorn thing go."

"But if she marries the mayor's son-"

"When. Wolflock. When she marries the mayor's son. If you can't contain yourself this evening and you're going to do harm to the reputations of Miss Thorn or the von Herren's, I will send you home early. Go and have fun. Make some friends. You're only fifteen Winters. Go and focus on what your peers find important. You may find the love of your life out there."

Mr Felen's smile returned, but his cold green eyes told Wolflock he wouldn't hear another word on the matter.

Wolflock stood frozen. Icy cold shock prickled through his skin like shards. His own father had dismissed him. Perhaps he hadn't seen how important this was. That had to be it. He was made too happy by the drink in the sitting room and he wasn't in his right mind.

He would just have to show his father how dire the situation was.

The music came to a close as the song ended and the dancers clapped. Wolflock saw his nemesis bounce into the room in her scarlet ball gown that attempted to cinch at her chubby waist and mask her dumpiness under bundles of shimmering cloth. The same cloth that was hand sewn by a local tailor she was about to put out of business.

His piercing blue eyes scanned her rapidly. Her cheeks were rouged by the cool air outside, she had no bag, and her arms were empty. Where had she stashed the documents? The folds of her dress hung in cascading semi circles like a giant red cake with gold leaf beads slung in each curve. But, one sat higher than the others. The curve was squarer. And it was in the perfect distance for her right hand to take hold of.

She has extra pockets in her dress.

Wolflock knew if she left this room, he'd be forced to physically approach her to end the plot and he couldn't stomach that. If he did it, everyone would accuse him of planting the evidence there. He had to have other people do it.

Everyone would have to see.

His eyes moved to the giant golden pumpkin the orchestra played from, towering over everyone at the ball. Without another thought he charged for the golden stairs in the shape of giant leaves, spiralling to the top. One of the dancing Autumn fae saw him come to the top of the glittering pumpkin and smiled. The wicked winged being wove its hands together and presented him with a large orange flower in the shape of a speaking trumpet.

"Entertain us, enthusiastic one," the fox-masked fae chuckled.

Wolflock nodded and accepted the flower with a cautious stare.

"Excuse me? Merry meet," he coughed, his voice booming clearly throughout the entire ballroom. The band stayed silent behind him and the room watched him, falling quiet in a wave he wasn't prepared for.

The only person moving was Aiirika Thorn. She glared her little piggy eyes at him as she wove between people, trying to reach the hallway across the huge room.

It was now or never.

"I have evidence that the Thorn family are about to destroy four key artisan industries in Plugh."

The room murmured but looked confused. Wolflock's father put his hand over his face.

"Under her top right fold in her skirt, Aiirika has secret documents she intends to plant on the mayor's desk in order to garner support for the building of four factories and farms that will destroy the work of scribes, alchemists, bakers and-"

"Get off the stage!" shouted one of the Thorn brothers while the other booed.

Their flunkies began joining in and the crowd

began to laugh. Wolflock scowled, but, as Aiirika was still permitted to move through the dancers, he knew he had to stoop to their level. These people may not care about what was really important, but they did care about their reputations.

"You boys should be the most concerned," he pointed to the Thorn brothers' snarky friends. "How long do you think this pair will prop your families up for when they can no longer service the community? Do you think for a moment they won't drop you with nothing and laugh about it?"

"Ah go blow steam somewhere else, Felen." Keinz sneered, pulling the Slarv twins with his tree trunk arms across their shoulders. "Just because you'll never know what it's like to be thick as thieves."

As he spoke one of the Autumn fae flew down and presented Keinz with another speaking trumpet. The room buzzed with delight at the confrontation and the grins from those around made Wolflock sick.

"You had the thick and the thieves correct, but not together. You're all thick and amongst thieves."

"Where's your proof?" Eiken tugged the speaking trumpet from his brother and cackled.

Wolflock's eyes narrowed. He hoped the trumpet was clear enough, so they absorbed every word.

"Where's your necklace, Keinz Thorn?"

The others all laughed, but Keinz' face fell.

"Don't worry, you haven't lost it. It was stolen. It's under your right hand, though."

Keinz' jaw dropped as he ran his fingers over Varush Slarv's collarbone to find his lost gold necklace with the thread of beads spelling out his name in the merchant's script.

Eiken paled, raising the trumpet to his mouth to speak, but no words came out. Miss Thorn also stopped, unable to get through the crowd leading back into the sitting room.

"Emotions are a silly thing. They lead to attachment, which is the source of all misery. You were so attached to that wild travelling merchant girl, promising her the world, and yet just last week she stopped returning you letters and said she was moving on early to the next province. Even you couldn't help but notice her wagon was still there, though. Ever wonder why?"

Varush Slarv grinned, but he shook his foxy head ever so slightly, glancing left and right for a way to escape. Keinz' face bloomed red, and he took a dangerous step towards the young man he was just holding.

"He's not the one you want. A bit of a stupid thing

to steal a necklace and stay around the person you'd stolen it from. He only has the necklace. It's his brother who is the reason for your missing letters."

"I-I didn't steal anything!" Varush stammered. "I promise, Keinz!"

"He's spouting his nonsense again. Drag him down and let's get back to having fun. His speeches are always so boring," his twin Venuck yawned, wiping his mouth with the back of his hand.

"Your merchant woman only uses a staining lipstick, doesn't she, Keinz? More commonly known as henna. It only rubs off when it's fresh and still damp, correct?" Wolflock said, ignoring Venuck.

Keinz looked warningly at the boy atop the golden pumpkin.

"Venuck has had a few drinks by now and he just wiped the makeup off his face. Is that the same shade of lip stain as is the colour of the goodbye note in your breast pocket?"

Keinz stared at the second twin in shock and outrage. His fists balled, and he went as red as his sister's dress.

"Of course, your secret would have been safe had you not told the only other man as desperate in the room to court transients as Nahten Worwest. Just this evening he cornered a poor girl, telling them he'd offer a merchant girl more status and stability, pursuing them 'more honourably than his friend'. He's the only who told your brother and sister of your transgressions."

"I would never!" Nahten gasped, although the two women behind him rolled their eyes. "This is poppycock! I keep any secret you tell me, Keinz! You're my oldest friend!"

"If he can keep a secret, I'm a pineapple." Wolflock laughed once before he continued. "What prospects can a woman bring into the nefarious Thorn family with merely looks alone? They couldn't have you foolishly bringing someone so lowborn into the family. Well... Miss Thorn can't. Eiken was simply mad that you were the one to lend his buggy to Furon."

Keinz turned to his brother. "Is... is that true? You kept Jarina from me because of a cart?"

"It's Aiirika's fault! She wouldn't lend him hers!" Eiken shouted, waving the speaking trumpet around like a flag of surrender.

"And the reason she wouldn't lend someone even a wheelbarrow to a race against her betrothed is that she knew he would destroy it!" Wolflock pointed a finger triumphantly. "She knew that if Rechen von Herren was racing against a hot head like Furon, her buggy would be annihilated. He's not only a terrible driver, as is evident by the marks on the wheels of his brand new phaeton, but he's also a cheat!"

The room was so silent, but you could cut the air with a knife. Aiirika glared back at him with her squinty hazel eyes.

"If she can tell he's a bad driver by the scratches on his vehicles, she can tell he cheats in other places too. No doubt his five lovers here tonight have not realised he's kept his coterie so close together. Most of them were in the audience of his escapades this evening. I do hope Miss Thorn informed you of the arrangement more than you informed her."

Rechen von Herren shrank down, glancing about for his mother to protect him.

"Even Aiirika Thorn wouldn't subject herself to the humiliation of being betrothed for much longer to a cretin of such low calibre, which is why right this very evening she seeks to procure her path to freedom and reap the rewards of seeds she will not have to nurture. Under the ruffle by her right hand you will find, Mayor von Herren, documents suggesting that the population of Plugh wishes to build four factories. This is a lie. Only the Thorn family and their benefactors wish for this, and it will destroy more than anyone could hope to gain from it."

Mayor von Herren stood beside Miss Thorn and looked at the chubby blonde girl with a mixture of exasperation and outrage. She held out her hand for what Aiirika had pocketed.

Wolflock held his breath. Would she fight it? Would she argue? He had her in such a tight corner, surely she couldn't escape.

Miss Thorn raised her arm into the air and summoned over an Autumn fae, who gave her a speaking trumpet flower. She looked around for a moment and Wolflock followed her gaze. She couldn't help but smile and he saw why. Her driver leaned cooly against the open courtyard doors, watching the spectacle with a smirk.

"Do you know why I would do such a thing, Wolflock Felen?" she said shrilly, pulling the documents from her skirt. He could tell she was doing her best to summon actress's tears. "It's because-"

Not wanting to give her a chance to spin a story away from his, Wolflock cut in. "You're in love with your driver and the only possible way you can be together is through complete financial independence."

The room audibly gasped and Aiirika's apple cheeks dropped. She looked to her driver through the crowd as the room broke into a hive of whispers.

"No." she began softly. "No. You are wrong, Mr Felen. You may have been right on most accounts, but on this, you are very wrong. My heart belongs to... has always belonged to..."

She kept her head down but Wolflock could tell she was glancing around for an escape.

"I'm so sorry, Mayor von Herren. My only wish when I accepted your son's hand was not to be his wife, but to be your daughter. You know I have no mother and I so hoped for you to be mine. But I am afraid my heart and hand belongs only to... Paretti Truls."

The ballroom descended into chaos. The Thorn brothers began shouting at their once friends, the other onlookers clapped and jeered depending on who summoned them here, Rechen backed away from his fearsome lovers, and Paretti Truls Junior looked lovestruck and dumbfounded.

Wolflock snarled, ready to counter her claims, but a pair of arms seized him and unbalanced him down the pumpkin stairs. His governess Gruta held his arm as she had when he was six, hauling him through the buzzing crowd as the orchestra started up at the Autumn court's behest. When he tried to use the speaking trumpet again she slapped it from his hand and into the trampling crowd.

"Wolflock!" she hissed, her eyes wide with terror. "You have no idea what you have just done! Your father told you! He told you!"

She trembled like a leaf and her eyes welled with tears. They made it into the sitting room and then the hallway leading back to the entranceway, avoiding the barrage of questions and stares from everyone gathering to gawk.

Two sets of guards blocked the doors, only allowing Gruta and Wolflock to pass. In the entranceway stood his sister holding hands with her best friend Ginia, his father and Mayor von Herren.

"...Falcon, I'm terribly sorry."

"Is there no other way to raise the resources?" his father pleaded. He had never heard that crack in the huge man's voice before. It made his spine feel like ice.

"With the volatile disgrace brought upon my name, my son's name and my office, no one would trust that this was not coercion. We won't be able to support the venture. Perhaps next year after things have been amended."

She handed back the silk scarf and ascended the stairs of the palace away from them without so much as a backwards glance.

"Father?" Myna whispered, resting her hand on

her father's arm. "What was that?"

Falcon Felen didn't move. "I proposed a new scientific venture to create a system of discovering where a person had been in order to resolve your mother's disappearance. That is no longer possible."

Ginia's green eyes filled with tears, and he rested her head on their father's arm. Wolflock couldn't move. He had just done a good thing. He had protected the town, weakened the Thorn's influence and saved the businesses he liked most. Why was no one celebrating?

"You cannot be serious? It's been eleven years!" he shook with fire. "Do you honestly think that anything we do will bring her back? Is that why none of you helped me tonight? You thought that some silly pipe dream of non-existent science would bring back a dead woman!"

Gruta, Ginia and Myna stared at him in variations of alarm; Gruta bored astonished disgust, Ginia gasped, and Myna glared with momentary hatred.

It was his father's words that broke his resolve.

"You ruin everything."

Not 'you ruined'. Not past tense. Present. Ongoing.

Wolflock's eyes stung with tears and he shouted, "Maybe I wouldn't ruin everything if you did anything!"

He charged from the room and snapped his

fingers at the valet, swallowing back his words as he tried to sound normal.

"Get me a horse for Owlet Street. The fastest you have. Put it under Felen."

A few moments later, Wolflock was mounted on a fresh chestnut stallion and galloping as fast as the wind would carry them. The night air chilled his tears against his wet cheeks, but he didn't slow down for a moment. People crammed the streets with Samhain celebrations, but he was having none of it. He drove the horse down the backstreets he knew would be empty, charging homeward until he saw the high gates decorated with lanterns over the bronze horses.

Instead of taking the horse to the front stables, he rode it around the back, still feeling the seething bitterness he had left the palace with. He leaped off the horse and tied it to the post where cab horses usually were tied so it could rest, eat and drink, and ran into the stable. Out of the fourteen stalls, he opened the door to the second left from the end.

"Wolflock?" the horse bayed.

Wolflock couldn't speak, but seeing his patchy white and brown stallion eased the pain in his heart.

Brennan laid on the ground with his four legs tucked in and a knowing gaze. "You didn't dance tonight?"

Wolflock knelt beside the horse and patted his shoulder before leaning into his side and sniffled. "No."

"You said you would dance."

"I said I would if I went. I didn't mean to go."

"You must dance later. Moving makes you happy. It makes me happy. Make sure you move."

Wolflock didn't answer, curling up against the warm horse as Brennan tugged a blanket over him. This was not the first night Wolflock had sought refuge sleeping in the stables, and Brennan knew it would not be the last.

CHAPTER 4
Expatriated

The next morning, Wolflock lingered in the stables with Brennan and the other horses until he got hungry. He was about to try to grab something from the kitchen when Gruta came down with a cheeseboard of his favourite snacks.

They were both alarmed to see the other.

"I knew you were down here when I saw the palace horse outside. I didn't know when you would come back up to the house, but I thought I'd give you some time to think about things."

Wolflock frowned as he took the platter. "Think about things? What things?"

Gruta sighed, giving Brennan an apple slice. "After last night... Wolflock, you need to consider how this has affected your family."

Wolflock looked away to chew.

"You brought public disgrace to some of the most powerful houses in Plugh. In the palace! You disgraced the mayor's son and suggested that she is gullible enough to be swindled into dealings that would devastate the town. Who would want to have any business with any of us anymore? We are a liability."

"*We* are a liability. You're just a servant. You'll be fine."

Gruta gripped her shawl above her heart and sat back. "I know you're upset, but if you would write an apology to-"

"You're not my mother, Gruta! You're my governess! Stop trying to be more than you are. If anyone here thought you were my mother, my father wouldn't be finding a fool's path to get her back!"

Gruta's expression grew cold and she rose to her feet. "Very well. If that's what you think of me. Merry part."

Wolflock felt a rock drop in his stomach, but he wouldn't apologise. No one could make him. He stubbornly refused to eat the cheese platter and lingered around the stables and the forest at the back of the estate for another full day. By dusk he felt grimy and in desperate need of a bath. Being dirty was far too distracting and Brennan had told him for the fifth time to apologise to Gruta, so he retreated back to the manor.

The staff all avoided his eyes as he made his way back to his room. He called for a bath to be run in his ensuite and took a long soak in lavender salts to eliminate his stress. It didn't work. Myna and Ginia swore by it, but the scent was too strong. The bitter sweet lavender turned the water lilac and the only pleasant thing about it was nudging the little florets into different shapes.

After a while he closed his eyes and leaned on the high back of the porcelain bathtub, sighing across the water as he tried to devise a way to get out of strife without having to apologise. He heard someone open his bedroom door and two pairs of feet came in. Tentative steps on the carpet creaked the old floorboards.

Two new staff, He thought, casting his mind into his room and forming an image of them. *Two girls. They're clinging to each other. They've been told to do something they're afraid to do. Moving over to my desk. Not touching it though. No drawers sliding. One moving to my bed. As she leaves her step is considerably lighter. She put something heavy on my bed. And now they're running from the room. They forgot to shut the door. Ah. They've remembered.*

Wolflock took a few more breaths and sank under

the water, curling into a ball where all the world was purely him and his heartbeat. He had no answers and he couldn't focus until he knew what the two servants had done in his room.

He dredged himself from the bath and dried himself with a fresh fluffy towel that sat folded everyday on his bathroom counter. He drew on his maroon bathroom robe and slippers, not even drying his hair as he couldn't wait any longer.

An open, empty trunk sat on his bed.

Are we going to Corl for Winter? We're leaving late in the season. Surely father wouldn't run scared from the gossip mongers.

He turned to his desk and saw three new pieces of folded paper on the polished mahogany. They were each for courses at the three major universities on the continent. Arcamedia in Shellinden Imperial City, known best for its courses in history, social sciences, law and art. Wu Dan in Shruiken, capital of Xiayah, provider of the highest grade philosophy, mathematics, technology and engineering. Mystentine in Shiriling, nestled atop the mountain that hugged the capital city of the same name.

He flicked open the Mystentine pamphlet with one hand. They promoted majors in architecture, science, biology, medicine and occult studies.

Wolflock's chest lurched. This wasn't a suggestion. His father had laid it out as clear as day.

Choose and go.

Anger flashed through his slender frame, and he threw the pamphlet away, running over to the bed and shoving the trunk off with all the force he could muster. He refused. He wouldn't do it. He would not let anyone send him away. He'd done nothing wrong. He'd saved the town and not a single person acknowledged it. Instead, he was being treated like a villain. He was being banished.

His very family had turned their backs on him as if he were a scab they itched to pick off and be rid of. He buried his face into the edge of his bed and screamed into the blanket.

The door opened without the entrant knocking. Without looking up, he shouted into the blanket.

"Get out, Myna!"

She kicked his door closed with her heel, telling him she carried something in her hands. "There you go again. Mffl, mffl, mffl," she tittered, and set the tea stand on his dresser before hoisting herself onto it.

Wolflock raised his head and snarled at her. "I said-"

"Did you pick one?"

"Father can't make me go to any of them. If I wanted to study, I'd go to the Grothien one outside of Delenstore."

"What? And learn how to be a priest or a farmer? I think not. I think you'd fit in more in Wu Dan."

"You're only saying that because you know I won't pick the one you suggest. You clearly want me to go to Arcamedia or Mystentine. I don't want to be corralled into classes I'm not interested in! I don't want to study."

Myna shrugged with a little squeak, then slowly poured herself a cup of tea.

"Perhaps. But you must stop lying to yourself, brother. You have always wanted to study. I don't know why you resist it. Imagine being surrounded by your peers of equal mind and enjoying exploring the depths and heights of science together? I can see you working on strange alchemies and creating new powders and tools to find all those clues you like. I also believe they've just announced a new psychology department that focuses on derangement and crime. I'm sure even you can glean new information from those who would otherwise present themselves as ordinary."

Wolflock squinted at her.

"This was your idea, wasn't it?"

Myna sipped her tea, avoiding his eyes.

"What are you not telling me?"

She kicked his dresser, leaving a particular red dirt mark on the polished wood. Her little shoes were walking shoes, and she'd been out and about that morning. Her pudgy feet were more swollen than usual. Sweat dampened her wrists where her now missing gloves doubled over. She had been to the post office and picked up the flyers for him.

"Why did you race to the post office today?" He stood up and looked her over. "Did father send you on an errand?"

She set her tea down and raised her nose at him. "He may have."

"And what was that?"

She didn't answer.

"He didn't plan to send me to university, did he?"

"Wolflock, you're just going to make yourself mad. If you pick a university to go to, then I'll be able to convince father to fund the expedition and give you an allowance. If you go raining flames on him, he may very well send you back to-"

She put both hands to her mouth and gasped.

"HE WAS GOING TO SEND ME BACK TO CORL!?" Wolflock roared, then paced feverishly around the room. "Myna, tell me he wasn't going to send me back there! I can take the simple atrocities that happen here, but to send me back there! Where all things are swindling, money and the obtuse politics. Am I to waste away under the endless, mindless dinner parties? Myna, he can't be serious!"

"Wolflock, ease your mind. I took care of it." Myna hopped down from the dresser and caught him by the sleeve. "You are not going to Corl. I wouldn't wish Aunt Liona's constant matchmaking on anyone, let alone my own brother." She took his thin hands in her squishy little ones and looked up sincerely into his eyes. "I have the letter hidden, but you have to make a choice. Please. Let me go to father with the news that you've decided to pursue a course of study. That way, you can go and find all the learning you could hope for."

"And the family can recover from the scandal I revealed last night."

Myna made a face that said she would have worded it differently, but let the disagreement rest. "I may be able to turn things around in our favour."

"Of course you can." Wolflock rolled his eyes. "If anyone can manipulate the strings of the political sphere, it's you, sister mine." He sighed, slumping in resignation. "You have to promise me that you will stop the Thorns and their ilk from ruining the city. There's not much to ruin, but take care of it while I'm gone."

Myna's face split into the happiest smile Wolflock had seen on her. She threw her arms around his neck and hugged him tight. "I will! I will make sure everything runs smoothly until you get back. Where are you going to study?"

Wolflock smirked sheepishly and opened a side compartment on his bedside table. Inside of it were old, tattered information booklets he'd had posted to him months ago.

"Mystentine of course. They have the closest course I could envision to improve my investigative skills. They also have the most experimental sciences and magics which could lead to increasing the ability to collect and refine data. They've also begun to engineer a reversed telescope. Instead of pointing it skyward to the celestial bodies, they have it turned back to the substances we see every day."

Myna's green eyes brightened as he opened the secret compartment of his bedside table. "Can mine do that?"

"I had a local carpenter make it as per my designs. It stopped Gruta from nagging me about what letters I was receiving."

"How long have you been planning this?" Myna

took up one of the university booklets and flicked through it.

Wolflock shrugged, waiting for his booklet back. "Brennan was the one who picked it."

"Your horse chose your university?"

"Literally. He plucked it out of my pocket when I rode back from the post office and insisted that I read it to him cover to cover. It became his bedtime story for a few months."

"You didn't answer my question."

Wolflock put the tips of his fingers together and leaned forward. "A while."

Myna fanned the pages of the booklet and saw the print date in the back cover. "A while indeed. If you wanted to go before last Spring, why didn't you say anything?"

"I didn't know how to ask father. It was after the issue with the princess's tiara and the donkey. Then... whenever I felt as if he would be receptive, something came up. It was just never the right time."

Myna nodded knowingly. "Well, now is the right time. How did you intend to travel?"

Wolflock opened the booklet to the second last page for a postcard tucked in the back. "The only way to get there this late in the season is by ship. All the mountain passes freeze up but there is one ship that can get over the ice."

"Is that the big pretty grey one with the silver wings, isn't it?"

Wolflock nodded. "The Silver Ice Hair. I may have to take a fast carriage North to catch it though. There's no way we'll make it on in time. It leaves tomorrow mid-morning."

"Oh that will be fine. It will cost a bit extra, but it will be fine."

"Myna, there is no possible way you will be able to convince father to pay for the trip, get supplies to the ship in time and have everything I need ready to go by mid-morning tomorrow. It's not logically possible."

"I beg your pardon, brother mine, but it certainly is. What do you think I do in my spare time? Lay about with politician's children playing marbles? Now, write a letter to the ship master and tell them we'll pay whatever is needed to gain you passage tomorrow. I'll come with you to make sure the transfer goes through. Father can reimburse me later." Myna stood up and paced, tapping her chin.

"You are saying words and I'm starting to think you've been toying with me this entire time. If so, I'll feel most annoyed that you tricked me into showing you my bedside table hiding spot." Wolflock said, half joking.

"I have a few investments that can pay for the resources the ship will need. I'm sure their particular shade of white sails are hard to come by. And every ship can do with extra stationary. Ink isn't cheap you know?"

"Investments? Myna! You're thirteen! What could you possibly-"

His sister stopped, smirked at him, then continued pacing. "Just a few local businesses who wanted a hand getting through particular legislation. I know the right ministers to give them help. Now I receive a regular share of their profits. It's only a little bit, but it's a steady stream."

Wolflock's mouth opened and closed a few times before he shook his head in disbelief. "I don't know why I'm surprised. Very well. If you think it's enough, I'll write the letter."

And with that the plans spiralled into motion. Wolflock sent his letter using Myna's crow to send word ahead to the ship and the dock. Myna came back to report that their father agreed to everything, and Wolflock packed his trunk with his necessary clothes, toiletries and savings. There wasn't room for his alchemy kit, musical instruments, or any of the books Myna recommended for prolonged travel.

Neither Gruta nor his father came to see him.

Wolflock barely slept through the night. Eventually after tossing and turning, he decided to go to the stables. He couldn't bear to let Brennan see him disappear on the ship. It would just be too hard. So he brushed him over and wrote a long list of preferences for the stable hands to abide by in his absence.

He woke in the grey dawn light to the carriage driver, Huston, gently shaking him awake.

"Master Felen, have you been down here all night? It's time to go, sir. The carriage is ready."

72

CHAPTER 5
The Beginning of the Journey

The city of Plugh slept through the misty hours of the morning. Not a creature stirred as the sun grumbled slowly into the sky, weary from the Samhain festivities and subsequent clean ups from the day before. The only movement came from the softly clattering mahogany carriage the Felen children rode within.

Without any other carriages to contend with, the Felen carriage made its way out of the city in an hour, coming along the main road to the docks.

The woodlands between Plugh and the Zilber river had turned from their usual emerald green to pale brown as Autumn nestled into the land. Trees shimmered with gold and yellow leaves as the animals gathered stores to prepare for the expected frost. The deer of Northern Grothener, who locals said brought tidings of abundance during springtime, were grazing peacefully along the tree line.

Wolflock and Myna watched in weary morning silence as the herd rubbed off clumps of their old brown fur, revealing their transformed snow white patches. They lifted their heads at the sudden noise of the single carriage clacking along the wide road.

A beautiful chestnut mare with a soft mulberry harness and no bit led it along the dusty road. The gold trim of the carriage ran along the door, windows and hand-carved decorative woodwork glittered in the sunlight.

Wolflock and Myna sat opposite one another, Myna looking eagerly forward at the oncoming scenery. Wolflock lounged across the plush seat, propped up by the corner of the back of the seat and window ledge, feeling a coldness in his chest as all he knew to be warm moved further and further away from him. He tried his best to keep his expression blank in case Myna started to look for any signs of hesitation. He couldn't help crossing his arms over his chest as the coldness burrowed into him. If Myna asked he could always blame the morning chill.

In contrast, Myna sat up taller and taller with every new thing that passed.

"The deer are already white. It's going to be a cold Winter. Shame. Warmer ones mean Ginia won't drag me out ice skating." She kept her dainty hands clasped neatly in the folds of her skirt.

Wolflock half wanted to say, "And heaven forbid anyone move you to a place you can't collect societal information," but the glimpse of the docks in the distance seemed to glue his tongue to the roof of his mouth.

"Oh, look at that! Lady Magreet's new spice shop is open. I'll see if she has curry leaves. Oh, and look! Mr Fusch caught a shark! Marvellous. The new fishing line must be a strong one."

When she became particularly excited by seeing businesses she intended to check on her way back, she ran her hands over her long, jet black hair that lay plaited over her shoulder and rested against the golden-brown shawl draped across her chubby frame. The brightening sunlight made her eyes an even more striking shade of acid green that analysed every detail of the passing landscape.

When she couldn't elicit a response from Wolflock from her exclamations, the only sound within the carriage became the agitated and irregular tapping of her small heeled shoes. The sound was like a mosquito buzzing around a sleeper's nose. Every time he settled into his brooding thoughts her tapping would jerk him back into the carriage.

"Myna, please!" Wolflock groaned and sat up in frustration. "Either kick the seat with a rhythm or stop. It's becoming irritating."

She turned her icy glare on her brother. "Well, Wolflock," she hissed, "I wouldn't have to irritate you if you'd let me know what's going on in that head of yours. I still can't believe you left father on such strained terms!" She maintained her glare, kicked the seat again in defiance, and haughtily raised her chin in challenge. "I've already promised the materials to the ship and now there is no guarantee he'll reimburse me!"

Wolflock stretched his arms out and fell back against the seat, raising a condescending eyebrow at his little sister's behaviour. He looked her over. Her hands were clenched in her lap so hard her fingers were going red and her jaw tightened. He could tell she was nervous about him leaving too. She was always such a talkative girl and his silence was agitating her. As she continued to glare, Wolflock conceded. He wouldn't admit it out loud, but he owed her.

"He was the one who refused to come down and

see me. Perhaps it's for the best, anyway. I'm sure he would have just stood there and said nothing," he finished bitterly.

Feeling his anger bubbling up inside him, he looked at his attire as if it was suddenly far more interesting than anything else in the carriage. He didn't want to snap at her. That would mean he'd receive no blessing for his travel from any of his family.

He brushed his nails against his black vest, careful to avoid the swirling, embroidered silver thread, then thumbed the dodecahedron cufflinks at the end of his white buttoned shirt. Even at a glance his family's wealth glinted through. The unmarred cloth with perfectly ironed creases down the legs and arms showed the high levels of care only the most wealthy families in Plugh were accustomed to. That, and the pristine white shirt were things Wolflock realised he may not see again for quite some time.

Catching his sister's goading eye again, Wolflock sighed and crossed his legs, resting his hand against the knee of his black slacks. The tension grew thick and he realised that, as long as she thought he would concede to her, she may allow the rest of the journey to the ship to be in peace. Keeping his face turned away, he bit his lower lip in thought. How could he make her smile while not forgiving his father? After a few moments, he lifted his gaze to meet hers in fond exasperation.

"I'll send you letters about all the people I meet. I'll also make sure anyone important has a favourable introduction in case you want to pursue any ventures up North."

Her expression softened, then the excitement of future prospects brought out an uncontrollable smile. He smiled in return and turned his gaze back out of the window, glimpsing his reflection.

Although his posture was relaxed, his piercing blue eyes shone with cold intelligence, planning ahead for how he would behave on the ship and what he may have to do if he couldn't get on.

He decided to try and be smiley like Myna would do, just until he could find the best people to study. With a few months ahead on an inescapable vessel with the same people, he hoped they would be interesting. If the letter hadn't reached the ship though, he may have to bargain with labour. Maybe they'd need a translator? Or possibly scribe. He would blatantly refuse to do any hard labour of course. His soft hands weren't made for climbing rough rigging and hauling barrels.

His long, slicked black hair just scraped the top of his shoulders despite it being a little long for the Plugian fashion, but he didn't care. He didn't much care what anyone thought anymore. At least no one from Plugh. He had finally deemed them all to be simple- minded socialites, whose lack of enthusiasm for intellectual pursuits were beneath his attention. Hence, his growing eagerness to escape the city and begin his studies. The further he rode away from Plugh, the more intense the conflict within him grew.

"Please write to father when you can. He will worry about your wellbeing. I know you feel like he deserted you and-"

"I'll write whenever the news is interesting," Wolflock huffed. "When he's calmed down, I'm sure he will be happy to receive my letters. After you've filtered them, of course."

Myna puffed out her cheeks crankily. "I wouldn't have to filter them if I knew you wouldn't try to sneak in unnecessarily passive aggressive comments. He's under enough stress trying to resolve the drama you've left us with."

"I see no drama. All I did was show the mayor's son to be immoral and unworthy of succeeding his mother after her term, and protected the town, once again, from the Thorn family."

"You broke up the most prestigious engagement in

front of the whole town at the Samhain festival, on the mayor's birthday, and then proceeded to inform everyone of his infidelity and cause a scandal that undermined every morsel of the mayor's authority. Though, I do suppose Miss Thorn's plans were sufficiently foiled, for now."

"They were fools if they hadn't already known. The signs were as plain as day. He was always arriving at public meetings with a distinctly brown shade of lipstick that could be noted on the mouths and necks of his male and female partners. That should have been the first give away, and his obvious lack of public affection should have been the second. As for the scandal, I still stand by the fact that I saved many of the city's best artisans."

"How could anyone but you have known, brother mine? His romantic business is his own, and you had no right to publicly shame him for it. As for the artisans, they don't even know who you are. You're just a customer. I just wish you'd been more subtle about it all."

"It was the only way I could get them to listen about his underhanded dealings with the Thorn family. His sudden increase in wealth as shown by his expensive new shoes, that racing wagon, and gaudy jewels. Had he been in office it would have been the Thorn family running Plugh and not the actual government office. I did the town a favour!"

"You'll never understand the game of politics. Events like this need to be handled with diplomacy." She shook her head and conceded the argument with a fond smile. "This is why I must rewrite your letters to father."

"Regardless, I am grateful to finally make this journey. There should be just enough time to get there before the passes freeze over. I have to thank you for saving me from being sent to Corl."

"Wolflock..." Myna rolled her eyes, "you would still find trouble in Corl, my brother. You crave it with every fibre of your being."

"That is hardly fair, Myna. I'd rather say that trouble craves me."

"Well, I hope your journey is neither too boring nor too dramatic, for neither would be good for father's health. It's still a shame you brought nothing to read and only your journal to write in, even after I offered you the contents of my library."

"And how would you have proposed that I carry any of your gigantic tomes, Myna? No. It is far more practical to leave such things behind and consider what lays ahead. Besides, there should be at least twenty people on the ship that I can study." He allowed a tiny smile to creep onto his lips.

"Well, it is the thought that counts, is it not?" Myna smirked.

"Aye. Which is why you should have thought."

They both snickered at their inside joke.

"This is exactly why you won't make any friends. You rebuke anyone trying to do you a kind turn if it doesn't suit your specific tastes. The same as always, my dear Wolflock," Myna sighed, sweeping her hand to her forehead in mock theatrics.

The siblings shared a knowing smile then resumed their earlier observation of the world outside of the carriage window with the tension finally dispersed.

As the sun crept higher in the sky they heard the sounds of cargo being loaded onto ships. The boisterous cacophony of crewmen shouting instructions to each other, clattering carts rolling over the cobblestone road, and merchants heatedly bartering flowed through the carriage as they neared the water's edge. Around them, children ran between workers, playing with colourful whirligigs and chasing down the cawing seagulls, their laughter intermittent with the splash of water along the wharf piles.

Seebruecke was the nearest dock to Plugh and, while it was not the largest in Puinteyle, it was convenient for those wishing to travel either North or South along the river.

It was easy to spot the ship Wolflock intended to board. The Silver Ice Hair stood out against the other, smaller, less ornate ships. The beautiful, pale grey hull, trimmed with silver, sported two great metal wings. Wolflock had chosen this ship in particular for its speed. Those silver wings granted the ship the ability to travel over the Silver Lake during Winter, preventing it from being stalled by the thick ice.

Myna leaned out of the carriage window to catch a better look at the magnificent ship as they approached, a bright smile dancing across her lips.

"I wish I could come with you!" she chimed. "But Ginia would be heartbroken. You know how she hates to be apart from me."

"Perhaps you can both come and visit me sometime." Wolflock took a breath and steeled his nerves, rising from his seat when the carriage pulled to a halt.

This was it. This was his first venture so far from home alone. He was taking real steps away from his hometown, the town he hated. Real steps to his independence.

His body felt numb and his mind raced too fast for even him to catch a thought. All he could focus on was one movement at a time.

He opened the door and stepped down from the carriage, and as the sun warmed his pale face his numbness blossomed into excitement. Freedom he'd never before experienced bobbed in the form of a great silver ship. He slung his satchel bag over his shoulder as Huston collected his trunk and passed it on to one of the dock workers to be taken onboard.

"Do you think father would let us come?" Myna asked as she descended beside him.

"You would have to ask him, but, I'm sure, if you had company and protection, he would let you." Wolflock took her hand to help her down. He glanced to Huston as he hopped back up onto his seat, waiting for Myna to depart back to the city.

"Merry part, Huston," Wolflock nodded, feeling a pang as he realised this may be the last time he saw the old man. One of the only people who had the same appreciation for horses as Wolflock. The old man taught him how to saddle Brennan so they were both comfortable, and he'd stopped the farrier from over charging him more than once for new shoes. Although simple, Huston had always been kind and helpful, to which Wolflock held him in better esteem than he held most people.

"And merry meet again, Master Felen," Huston nodded back, drawing in his lips over his few remaining teeth as he suppressed tears. Of sadness or relief, Wolflock wasn't sure, but he hoped the old man thought his apple sneaking, bridle tampering, and pedantic instructions were fond memories.

There was nothing else to speak about, but, yet, it felt like there was so much left to say. Wolflock felt like he could spill all manner of appreciation on Huston, but he doubted anything beyond two syllables would mean anything to the man. He turned towards the dock and held his breath, steeling himself for the next step. Was he ready?

He looked back once more and smiled as he saw Huston leaning down and talking to the horses as if they were work colleagues.

At least someone will take good care of Brennan while I'm away.

Myna pulled Wolflock towards the long wooden dock, excited to see the ship up close. She took his arm as they entered the throng of twenty people standing together behind the smooth railing.

Wolflock could tell, by the distance of the people from the boat, who had been on the ship from Corl or longer, and who were newly boarding. Like Myna, those staring eagerly at the ship had not been on it for a month and a half, while those standing further along the dock clearly were in need of time on solid land.

The ship was magnificent to behold. Wolflock thought knowing the dimensions and layout would give him an idea of what to expect, but, in person, the sailing ship took away his breath. It was a little under fifty yards long and fifteen yards wide and the whole ship looked like a giant, silver knife ready to slice through the water. There were three masts on the deck, the centre one being the largest and supporting a crow's nest at its peak amidst bundles of white sails.

Wolflock glanced around to see who could give him any information about their departure, but, as everyone looked equally perplexed, he decided to approach the nearest person to them. A lady dressed from head to toe in black, with a small child intrigued with something in their large travelling sack stood a small way back from the crowd.

Wolflock wanted to start his journey on a better foot than what he'd left Plugh in, so he took a moment to analyse the woman and gauge what was the best way to approach the conversation. Her auburn hair was coming free from her poorly tended bun as she dabbed her eyes with her frayed handkerchief. Her dress was sun faded and her shoes old and worn, all suggesting that she had come from a working family and had travelled far to make this journey.

With single-minded focus, the small child dug through the bag, sifting through new luxuries they had purchased on the dock. She shared the same, distinct auburn hair as her mother and seemed unperturbed by her mother's distress.

"My condolences," he said solemnly, startling the woman.

"P-Pardon?" she hiccoughed.

"You've recently lost your husband, yes? Hopefully, you can recuperate on the ship. When will we be boarding, do you know?" He tried to appear pleasant and offered his fresh handkerchief to dab her eyes.

"The first mate should be out shortly to allow us on board, but things have been quite disorganised since we boarded. I don't believe we've met... or, have we, and I just can't remember you? My memory has been so slippery since the Justice took Artin... I was so thankful it took him quickly. He was a good man..."

Wolflock frowned and looked to Myna, who was watching the child. The Justice was a plague in the West that caused the victim to fall into a delirious state, where they felt the impact of all the pain that they had caused in their lives. You could only pray that your loved one died with haste and that their punishment would be short-lived. There was no known cure.

It was said to have come from the ancient ruins of Chaysaile City when the evil king died a thousand years ago. It wiped out thousands of people in the country Chalongesh and was said to be retribution for the war they wrought upon the continent. No one yet knew how it spread, regardless of the ongoing research at medical facilities in the West.

"I'm sure he was a good man," Wolflock replied, feeling awkward that she had replied by telling him about her husband, rather than being surprised that he'd guessed correctly.

Thankfully, the exchange was ended by a tall man with long, greying hair emerging by the gangplank above them and thumping his fist on the railing. He looked down with a frosty glare.

"Merry meet, all!" he shouted, not so merrily. "Welcome to the Silver Ice Hair. I am first mate Slavidus Oncor, for those who are joining us. I ask that all previous passengers board first and enter your rooms so that the new passengers can locate cabins that are not occupied. Mark off your names as you board." He held up a thick red book as two-thirds of their company shuffled back onto the ship, each placing a cross next to their name in the register as they boarded.

Wolflock's stomach fluttered as he realised he was about to embark on the biggest journey of his life. He was leaving behind all that was familiar to him and being thrust into a new world. He wouldn't have his father or Plugh to restrict him. Finally, he could reach his highest potential. The sense of impending freedom felt terrifying and exhilarating at the same time.

His stomach jolted again as the first mate called out the first name of the five people remaining on the dock. He was suddenly oblivious to the surrounding people, caught in his own immediate senses and thoughts.

The hard wood beneath his feet held him steady but knowing he was about to step off that made him shake. He never thought life could change so quickly. He never knew taking strides to his dreams would taste so bittersweet. What if it was all for nothing? What if the university rejected him the same way every school and tutor he'd ever dealt with had done? What if the people on the ship became so unbearable he threw himself overboard? He'd have to live in the forests and mountains never to see society again.

As if she could feel his anxiety, Myna interlocked her fingers with his and hugged his arm as the man calling the names asked for the second person on the list.

Wolflock clenched his jaw and steeled himself, then hugged his sister tightly, unable to remain still. As much as they fought, he still loved her and nothing would take that away.

But what if this was it? What if he never saw them again? His final words had been in anger to his father. What if they were all he was remembered by?

"Tell father that I love him and that I will miss him," he swallowed, as he hugged her hard to his chest, feeling her nod of assent. He squeezed her upper arms as he heard his name being called. "And know that I love you too and I await your visit as soon as possible."

"I will make preparations shortly, brother mine," she sniffed and he could feel her trembling. "Promise me you'll *try* to stay safe. At least until you get to the university where they can keep an eye on you."

"What's this now? No tears," he wiped her overflowing eyes with his thumbs. "How can I give you instruction on how to continue my legacy of foiling the Thorn plans and making Gruta's hair even more grey if I'm not safe? You're smarter than tha, Myna."

"Wolflock F. Felen!" the second mate shouted again from the top of the gang plank.

Wolflock gave Myna a reassuring smile as he

released her, finding that keeping his little sister happy distracted him from his own anxieties, "Make sure the city knows a lone Felen is just as dangerous as multiple of us. And keep the good apples for Brennan. And leave my room alone. And keep me informed of any new book releases! And-"

"Go!" she laughed through her tears as she gave him the last push he needed, and he ascended the ramp onto the ship with his head held high.

Rhiannon D. Elton

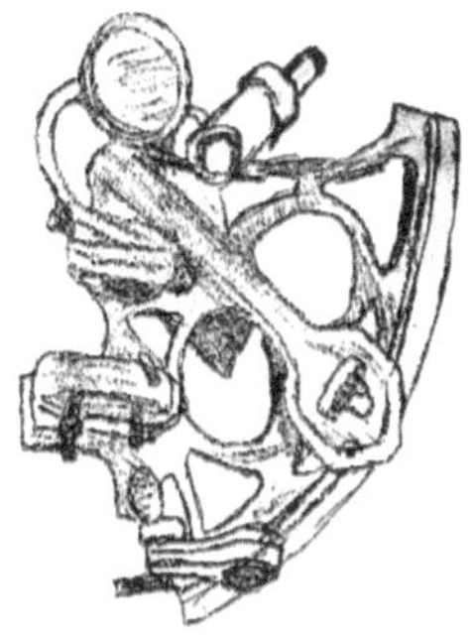

CHAPTER 6
Mischief Magnet

As he reached the deck, he had a moment to see the man calling out the names up close. He was a tall man, muscular and tanned from living on the ship, but something etched his face with aggravated exhaustion. Wolflock briefly wondered what had caused it, but, as First Mate Slavidus called the next two people up, a pair of burly sailors ushered him under the deck. He turned one last time before descending and waved to Myna, thankful for the distance as any words he had were caught in his throat. She beamed up at him and waved her handkerchief in farewell between dabbing her eyes.

Wolflock descended below into an elegant hallway

with a row of doors on either side, trimmed with silver filigree and decorated with nautical paintings. It was lit by fairy dust lanterns, one mounted between each door and two at either end. Their normally vibrant light had dimmed and settled, but a good shake would brighten them up again. The doors were all open so the passengers could see which cabins were taken.

Wolflock caught sight of the agitated faces, sharp hand movements, and frustrated fidgeting from the folk conversing. There was not a single smile amongst the passengers and Wolflock began to worry that the Silver Ice Hair was not the extraordinary passenger ship the brochures made it out to be. He peeked into each room he passed, looking for his lodgings.

Whenever Wolflock had stayed in hotels or various venues his father had taken them to, the staff would always show them their key and escort them to their residence and then hand over the key as a gesture of good faith the room was fresh. There were no such pleasantries here.

He bumped into the back of one of the crewmen who had stopped due to congestion in the hall. Several of the crew were still trying to get empty crates and barrels from the hull onto the dock, even though they were moments from launch, blocking the way. Wolflock couldn't proceed, so he continued peering into the open rooms at the occupants. He glanced at a man in his thirties reading on his bed and saw the man put down the book after staring at the page for a few seconds, sigh, then look at the same page again. Wolflock noted the wooden frames of several rectangular canvases leaning on his wall, each individually tied with stockings holding protective sheets of cloth.

A fabric used to protect only the most delicate items. I wonder if it's to stop semi dried paint from smudging, Wolflock thought. Gruta had offered her old stockings when he was a child and all he would eat were tomatoes. She'd shown him that the thin fabric, when beyond the use of clothing anymore, was great for storing onions, tying back plant vines without bruising them, and separating liquids from sand and soil. Regret caught him around the throat again. Normally by now he would have made amends with Gruta for snapping at her, but he'd never separated her from their family. She had raised them in the absence of their mother. He knew it hadn't been easy. He never aimed to make it easy. But he didn't enjoy seeing her upset like that. Frustrated at his shenanigans, worried about his experiments, exasperated at his stubbornness. All of those were fine. But disappointed in him. That stuck with him longer than he liked.

The crewman in front of him pressed themselves to the wall and allowed the larger items to pass, allowing him to continue further down the hall.

I'll have to get her something nice to make up for everything. She needs a softer set of things for her hair. The current one keeps breaking hers and leaving fly away strands. Maybe I'll find something enchanted in Mystentine for her.

In the room next to the painter, he saw two dark-skinned women talking in low tones and glaring at anyone who passed their doorway. One bounced her knee as if she was anxious to leave. When the one with tightly bound rows of hair caught his eye they both fell silent and stared at him until he moved on.

Beyond them, a Xiayahn family of four sat in silence with their heads bowed. The eldest was a stern-looking gentleman with what appeared to be his three children. A girl a little older than Wolflock and two boys much younger than her. Wolflock wondered if they were in some kind of prayer. His eye was drawn to her finger, tracing down the column of strange symbols written on the bamboo booklets on their laps. As she turned the pages at lightning speed, it became clear that she possessed a remarkable reading speed.

Educated and disciplined. He nodded in approval before moving along.

Next to their room, a husband and wife were sitting on the edge of their bed whispering to one another. They spoke in hushed tones to disguise their argument, but Wolflock could see they were quite upset due to their jerky hand gestures and furrowed brows.

Finally, he passed a room where a boy his own age lay back on his bed while looking at the roof, humming a cheerful song to himself. His left leg was propped on his right knee, and the dangling foot rocked in time with the tune. The boy had a large canvas bag with no other possessions or luggage to be seen. It sat by his bed and Wolflock thought it may contain everything he owned.

How odd... he didn't board here, and he's not getting off for a few weeks at least... Why are his things still packed?

He finally came to the only empty room out of the twelve rooms in the hallway. As this deck only had passengers in it, he assumed the crew slept on the second level and that all the cargo would be kept in the hull to help balance the ship so it didn't turn belly up.

After a quick survey of his room, he measured it to be roughly six feet wide and eight feet long with a single simple side table bolted into the floor under the porthole window. The bed didn't look as comfortable as his one at his father's estate, but it would have to do. Above the bed was a shelf and a cupboard with a pillow and a thick blanket too big for the space it was stored in. He was relieved to see a small desk and a sturdy chair to write at. He tossed his satchel bag on it for now.

Wolflock opened the window and grinned as he spotted Myna, who was still standing on the dock, awaiting the launch of the ship. She waved with excited enthusiasm when he popped out of the window, making them both laugh.

It would be an impressive send off if she saw me on the deck. I'm barely a few feet higher than her here, Wolflock thought, wondering when they'd be allowed up.

He heard the first mate's soft shoes 'fwump'ing down the stairs and he moved out into the hallway to catch him. Most of the other crew he'd seen were shoeless. The cranky older man appeared distracted, but Wolflock wouldn't let that deter him from seeing the ship launch.

"Excuse me?" he asked.

Slavidus started and grunted in annoyance, flicking his long grey streaked ponytail over his shoulder.

"What do you want, lad? I have places to be." He folded away the register of passenger names that he was still carrying.

The first mate was a tall man in his forties with a short, greying beard wrapped around his strong chin that was looking a bit scraggy at present, but the lines of his facial hair said that it was usually well kept. He was wearing fine hessian trousers and a sailor's suit shirt with the buttons fastened in the wrong holes. Both garments were shades of grey offset by his shiny brown leather shoes.

Probably acquired on their last stop for supplies. I wonder if he's colour blind. I didn't expect the executive crew to be dressed in such a slipshod manner. Wolflock pondered on the odd choice of attire. It was also evident from the bags under his eyes that whatever was upsetting him and causing his wardrobe malfunctions had endured for at least a fortnight. He's only seen bags that big in Gruta's eyes when he had fallen ill with a week long cold, only to immediately have Myna fall ill after him.

"I'd like to go upstairs to watch the ship start its journey."

"No," he grunted and pushed passed on his way down the hall.

"But why not?" Wolflock frowned and followed him, undeterred.

"The Captain is indisposed, and I can't watch

everyone. You'll all get underfoot and we'll be late. Now, get back to your room and you'll be told when dinner is ready. Now, everyone, stay in your rooms! Back now! I don't want to see any doors open!" he barked.

Wolflock stood dumbstruck for a moment, then scoffed, "Rude."

Slavidus hurried off faster to lose Wolflock, who grumbled as he retreated to his room. The other passengers were listening and had perked up at the request, but, as Slavidus dismissed it, they slumped back into their rooms. It was clear by the quiet dejection of the other passengers that this had become the norm on the Silver Ice Hair. The obedience and passivity of the other passengers irritated Wolflock. He wouldn't fall into such a stupor. He wanted to watch the ship launch. He was going to enjoy it and no one was going to stop him.

Once Slavidus was out of view, Wolflock glanced surreptitiously up and down the hall. The coast was clear. He closed his door so it would appear that he was in there, and dashed towards the stairs that led up to the deck.

He was going to watch the ship take off, regardless of what that grouchy old man said. But, just as he reached the stairs, he felt a yank at the ankle of his slacks and he tripped, falling forward. He snarled over his shoulder and saw the boy from the room next to him grabbing his pant leg.

The absolute gaul! Is he some kind of ship urchin? Is he part of the crew and I missed it? Wolflock glared at him, trying to look for details, but he couldn't tell. The boy had a slight tan from being in the sun, his hands were firm and calloused, but across the index and thumb where a knife in the kitchen was common. There were no other signs of frequenting a kitchen, though. He was far too slight to be hauling barrels. Why had this strange boy stopped him?

Before he could curse his assailant, the boy gave a devious grin and covered his mouth.

"You want to watch the ship take off, don't you?" he whispered in a thick, South Chalongesh accent. Wolflock nodded but his frown didn't budge.

"Well, going that way is only going to get you on scrubbing duty. Follow me."

He darted off down the hall in the same direction as the first mate, waving for Wolflock to follow.

Stopping two-thirds of the way down, he pulled a shell ornament on the wall and dropped a square flap from above them. It opened into a brightly lit room on the deck above.

"The ship is full of these fun secrets," the boy

smiled with a face full of cheek.

They scrambled up as quietly as they could, finding themselves shrouded in a clean white cloth under a long claw footed dining table. The other boy closed the trapdoor with a soft click and left it only half latched. Wolflock realised that this was also their escape plan and that the hatch didn't open from this side.

He's done this before, Wolflock thought.

The boy brushed back his dusty blonde hair and peeked out from under the tablecloth. He slipped out, waving for Wolflock to follow him as he tiptoed to across the planks. With the utmost care and precision, the blond boy stepped silently across the floor in his worn leather shoes. Wolflock saw he didn't tie the laces like normal people, but tucked them under the tongue.

"Watch out for the creaky ones. Everyone downstairs will know we're up here if you stand on them," he warned.

"And how am I supposed to know that?" Wolflock scoffed.

"You'd have to watch carefully, I expect."

He glided through the air and landed on a plank four feet away without a sound. Wolflock raised his arms and mouthed, " *What?!*", but the other boy just beckoned him forward.

"I'm sure you'll be fine. Come on. It's easy."

Wolflock didn't jump with nearly the same agility, choosing instead to reach across one toe at a time until he found solid ground again, under the scrutinising eye of his new acquaintance. The other boy leaped ahead, his movements so dainty and fluid that Wolflock thought he looked like a nimble deer bounding onto stepping-stones. He made it to the double doors without a sound and waited for Wolflock, who stumbled and looked more like a bulldog trying to avoid rat traps. However, he made it to the door with no obscenely loud creaks, and they found themselves both standing awkwardly nose to nose on a decorative plaque of bronze set in the wood floor.

"So," the shorter blond boy raised an eyebrow with a suggestive grin, "are you ready to take the next step in this relationship?"

Wolflock scowled and shoved him away, nearly toppling backwards off the plaque.

Laughing, his companion opened the door and peeked out. "We've got to time it just right..." Wolflock craned his neck to see passed him. "Get ready for when they pass... now!"

Keeping low, darting out of the room, he ducked behind some barrels in the sunshine of the top deck.

Wolflock quickly followed, nervous about being caught. He was unfamiliar with the layout of the cargo on the top deck and at ever turn he thought a crewmate would come around and spot them. The embarrassment of being the potential cause of that made him more determined to stay hidden. The pictures of the Silver Ice Hair didn't show any thing being stored on the deck. He wondered if they were really so disorganised that nothing was where it ought to be.

They crept behind barrels and crates, waiting for the bustling crew to pass as they prepared the sails to unfurl. Wolflock was grateful for being on the deck and in the fresh air, but he wasn't particularly impressed with the view of barrels, crates, and no shoreline scenery.

"This isn't it? Is it?" he scoffed. "We're not just going to run about the deck like naughty children, are we?"

"This is our warmup. Had to test you and see if you could be quick enough. C'mon!"

Wolflock gawked indignantly as the other boy continued their covert journey, slipping like bilge rats between the cargo not yet taken to the hull until, finally, they came to the rigging that led up the central mast to the crow's nest. "They made it easy for us. This is the tricky bit. I hope you're a fast climber."

Wolflock lost sight of his cheeky grin as he scaled up the rigging in a flash.

Idiot! We're bound to get caught! He looked around, sure someone would see them.

He debated with himself for a moment. His family had paid the Captain very well in ink, hemp and supplies, so it was unlikely he'd be thrown off the ship. Perhaps he'd just have to write lines or get a firm reprimand. Nothing he hadn't handled before... and the view was sure to be magnificent from up there...

Without another thought, he scrambled up, trying not to get his feet tangled as he raced after the other boy on the rough spun rigging. He waited to hear one of the crew shouting out after them, but, to his pleasant surprise, he heard nothing but the wind.

They must be too busy with what's in front of their noses...

Finally, he reached the crow's nest and fell into the oversized bucket. His body protested against the hard surface beneath him, but also refused to move for a few moments as he caught his breath. The other boy offered him a hand, which he begrudgingly took hold of, and was hoisted into the wooden cradle.

"Thanks," he grumbled as he picked himself up and dusted off his trousers.

"You'll be thanking me again in a moment." The other boy winked and looked down over the edge, watching the oblivious crewmen.

Wolflock eyed the boy, but, before he could try and decipher his meaning, the sail rose up before them, coming to life as it filled with the strong river breeze. With a sudden jolt, the boat creaked and leaned forward.

He looked to the dock to see Myna waving in earnest up at him; he waved back triumphantly. *This* was how he wanted to be remembered. Standing at the highest point of this shining, albeit disorganised, vessel as he sailed on to heights Plugh could never offer.

The crew raced around the ship and untied the sails, letting them drop and catch the wind, pulling the whole ship as far forward as the anchor would allow. The crew shouted to each other and ran about, disorganised as some ropes flew about loosely in the wind, causing the ship to jerk.

The first mate came back on deck and took the wheel on top of the dining hall, shouting orders and steering the ship away from the shore. The other three sails unfurled, and the water below reflected their magnificence like a celebratory parade of sparkling confetti. Two men jammed poles into ·the capstan and began winding it, pulling the anchor from the depths of the river. The whole ship soared forward and Wolflock appreciated the web of ropes around the ship and what purpose they appeared to serve, much like the mental web he held of Plugh and all the clues and people within it. The ship increased in speed and sliced upstream through the centre of the broad river.

Every inch they departed further from Plugh, the fear of the unknown melted into excitement until all he was left with was the elation that the future held in store for him.

His journey had truly begun.

108

CHAPTER 7

Found and Boiled

"I'm Mothy." Wolflock jumped as the other boy nudged his elbow. "what's your name?"

"Wolflock Felen. A pleasure to meet you Mothy." he smiled, taken from his thoughts. The view and adventure had proven Mothy to be a rather convenient acquaintance. His playful nature, while somewhat disrespectful, had entertained Wolflock enough that he deemed Mothy a suitable subject for further study. The only people who had forced him to interact with them the way this boy had done was to make fun of him. This boy had no one to impress, so Wolflock cautiously gauged his interest was genuine.

"It's really amazing isn't it?" Mothy exhaled, gazing at their view of the river.

"It's definitely fascinating," Wolflock agreed and took in the shore on either side of them. The occasional patch of spruce trees and cobbled road streaked through the long grassy banks. It looked very much like the landscape paintings Wolflock often sat by in the library. "How long will it be until we get to Mystentine? I'm sure you're excited to arrive as well."

"How did you know I was going to Mystentine?" Mothy blinked in surprise and then smirked. "Have you already been spying on me? I didn't realise I was so fascinating."

He stretched his arms out, pushing off the rim of the crow's nest and held his hands out as if he was using his fingers as a picture frame for the scenery. "The first mate told me it will be a month or so until the Hatfjorn Lake and then another month by carriage to Mystentine."

"I'm glad it will only be two months, although I think it will be freezing by the time we get there." Wolflock paused, noting Mothy watched him keenly as he waited for his explanation. "I knew you were going to Mystentine because you're young, you're alone on the ship, and you aren't running around with the crew, so you don't work here. You had your whole life in the bag by your bed and you hadn't just arrived, so, knowing you have to depart eventually has stopped you from unpacking and making yourself too comfortable. You also seem quite bright. The only place you could be heading from here with all of that is Mystentine. You could be going for a new career, but I saw no tools of a trade, so, logically it would be more likely you're going to study at the university."

"Truly?" Mothy laughed. "That's fascinating! You got that all from a bag by my bed? You've got a sharper mind than I gave you credit for! I bet you get into all kinds of trouble."

"Yes... I just think of it more as a different way of seeing things." Wolflock gave a nonchalant shrug but couldn't hide his pleased grin, finally in the company of someone that appreciated his observational techniques, even if they hadn't been immediately evident. He couldn't blame the other boy for not being as observant as him.

For a long while, they pointed at the antics of the crew at work and at animals on the shoreline, all while enjoying the fresh river breeze. Birds flitted across the wide river, some diving down to catch fish, others sifting for bugs and crustaceans by the banks. A small herd of boar stopped drinking and playing the muddy bank to watch the ship before a whistle called them back into the trees. Fish excitedly swam South, splashing in and out of the water as they retreated to warmer places for Winter. For all of the pictures and paintings Wolflock had seen, nothing matched the animated beauty of the scene he moved through. The enchanting orange leaves against the blue water were a contrast made more beautiful by their temporary nature.

Wolflock began to wonder if the passengers would be allowed to enjoy the top deck at all on this journey when he felt a strong hand grasp his collar.

"Oi!" barked a gravelly voice, "you ain't s'pose to be up 'ere!"

One crewman had come up to watch for rocks in the water and had discovered their hiding place.

"Aw! C'mon, Grogen! He wanted to watch the launch! It's his first time on a ship!" Mothy complained as they both struggled for freedom from the man's monstrous grasp. He was clearly a Corshman, judging by his unrefined accent and the fact that he lifted Wolflock a good foot off the ground. Most of the people native to central and Eastern Shiriling were called Corshfolk as it was the previous capital before Mystentine City and they still resembled the six foot tall, muscle bound folk that could survive in that desolate climate.

"Tell ya what," he grinned a little wickedly and pulled them in closer to his dark red beard, "you 'elp me cook later, and I won't take this to the Cap'in."

"Deal!" Mothy grinned and extended his hand as if he were shaking for a business deal, his feet still dangling in the air.

"What!?" Wolflock's jaw dropped. "Wait! I didn't agree to that!"

"'E agreed for ya!" Grogen laughed and dropped them both.

Wolflock scowled, picking himself up from the floor again, dusting off his sleeve with a sharp flick of his wrist. He wanted to argue, but Mothy had already started climbing down and he knew his chances of success were slim without backup.

They had to climb down because Grogen's broad frame took up the whole crow's nest. As they reached the bottom he called out to another crewmate standing just behind the stairs, trying to stay out of sight.

"Hognut! Make sure they get back to their rooms, eh?"

"Alrighty... well ya not stowaways... uh... git back to ya rooms," said a stumpy brown-haired crewman, looking uncomfortable that they were disturbing him smoking his pipe. Judging by his shoulders rounded forward and the way he shook the matches out before he could light his pipe, Wolflock could tell he was looking forward to that smoke, but felt guilty about taking a moment to rest.

"Rude," Wolflock put his nose in the air as the crewman ushered them back to their rooms. He stood a few steps down and continued to try and light his pipe, taking a long draw before glancing at the boys heading into Mothy's room. He only stopped watching once he was sure they were inside and staying in.

They both lurked in Mothy's room as it was nearer to the stairs, giving them the chance to sneak out again if they wanted to. Mothy flopped on his bed and laughed at Wolflock scowling back at the door. "What's the problem? We'll be back out soon. It's just setting the table and serving food. Nothing too hard."

"Isn't that staff business?" Wolflock retorted. He was certain his father had paid more than enough for his passage so he did not have to endure menial chores.

"Oh, I get it now." Mothy groaned, his tone mocking. "You're royalty! It all makes sense now."

"What makes sense? I'm not royalty."

"Only royalty have staff, right? Or dress as richly as you?" He chuckled and ruffled his blond hair. "I guess I'm showing my upbringing a bit. We did do the wrong thing though. It's only a night. He could have asked us to do it all week."

"They're doing the wrong thing by keeping us shut in down here!"

"Are you always this stubborn?" Mothy laughed.

"Are you always so cheerful?" Wolflock glared in retaliation.

"Yes," they both answered in unison and broke out into fits of laughter.

Wolflock had never met anyone he felt so at ease with, and yet still so curious about. There was something contagious about his cheer and optimism and it made Wolflock want to know why. The boys spent the rest of the day together in Mothy's room, talking about the things they'd seen in the crow's nest and planning how they could sneak out again. They had long forgotten that they were to help with dinner until Grogen came and collected them at sunset.

"C'mon, ya little blighters. Time ta work."

The kitchen was positioned in the dining hall on the starboard side of the ship, half cordoned off by the benches the meals were served on. Intricate mosaics of river scenery tiled the area, keeping it safe from damage caused by spills. A huge iron cauldron sat in the centre of the U-shaped benches, bubbling with hot water and lentils.

"The most important thing about cooking here is keeping fire only on the tiled area, or else the whole ship could go up in smoke," Mothy said in an experienced tone with a hint of optimism. "That's what Grogen told me last week when I got caught sneaking around the ship."

"Mmmm...." Wolflock hummed, pulling a face at the fire that seemed to threaten him personally, "and... ah... it is safe enough to stop the ship from setting on fire?"

"Haha! Oh, you're funny, Lockie!" Mothy chuckled.

Wolflock cocked his head to the side as he realised Mothy hadn't called him by his proper name.

"Put these on," Grogen grunted as he tossed two stained aprons at them before Wolflock could make up his mind about how Mothy addressed him.

Wolflock glanced around as he held the apron at arm's length. He reluctantly copied Mothy, who threw the singed apron loop over his head and tied it around his waist. His face screwed up with the distaste of the dirty apron touching his clean vest, but at least it would stop any future food splatter from touching his fine shirt.

"Aye, Mothy, you start chopping and ya friend can

set the table, the utensils are in 'ere." Grogen kicked the cupboard to his right.

"Yes... set the table... ummm...." Wolflock had paid attention to the beautiful silver and gold ware at his own home, but the brass implements he was faced with were crude in comparison, and the wooden bowls hardly resembled the finely crafted porcelain he was used to. For the average person, the cutlery may have been considered high class, but, to Wolflock, they were mediocre at best.

"This is a bowl, aye?" he asked, holding up one of the wooden objects.

"That's a cup, my prince," Mothy laughed and pulled out some flatter objects and cutlery. "This is a fork, and this one is a knife. Put this on the middle and these two on the right if you would, your majesty."

"I know how to set a table," Wolflock lied indignantly and snatched them out of his hands. He had never had someone beneath his station talk to him like that before. It was so fresh. He didn't know how to respond.

"Oh! I thought you may never have had the opportunity to do it before in your chateau," Mothy said with a grandiose bow with flourishing hands.

"I'll have you know it is a *manor*. Chateaus are far too much maintenance," Wolflock retorted, deciding to play along with the mock snobbishness since it helped to ease the discomfort of the situation.

"Oh, forgive me, my prince. Us peasant folk may choose between the barn and the cottage. I personally choose the barn for the cottage is far too much maintenance. With all those windows and a hearth. Who wants any of those burdens?"

Wolflock couldn't help but laugh. Something about Mothy's wit and humour gave the air a mischievous glow. When he set out for his independence, he hardly thought his first introduction would be to learning that there were people out there that didn't play by the rules. The prospect of learning which rules could be bent and broken without causing the same levels of offence he normally did excited him.

He laid out the cutlery and plates and kept a close eye on the fireplace, glancing back at Mothy, who had began chopping up vegetables and fresh Plughian spices. His mincing motion was rhythmic, and his hands seemed to dance as he occasionally spun the knife in his hand.

Grogen's only task appeared to be stirring the cauldron and listening while Mothy continued to chatter about which spices worked with different vegetable medleies as if he were a master chef, pouring root vegetables into the pot. When Wolflock had finished setting the places at the dining table, he stood by Mothy and observed how differently he treated the food to the kitchen staff at his father's estate.

"I know it's above a servant to ask, but did you want to try? The breath down my neck has an air of curiosity." He offered the handle of the knife to Wolflock with a toothy grin.

"I.... uh... I don't..."

"You've never prepared food before?" Mothy whispered when Grogen began singing to himself. "Don't worry. I won't tell anyone you can't cut straight."

Wolflock's face flushed and Mothy grinned even more.

"Just copy me." He handed over the blade and took up another.

For the next hour, Wolflock copied Mothy as best he could while Grogen chuckled to himself, thinking of how the boy of wealth and prestige could so easily be taught from the one who had nothing but the clothes on his back. Wolflock would have normally been irritated by the labour, but learning alongside his new acquaintance made the embarrassment ebb away, only to be replaced by the determination to be able to match Mothy's skill. He made it look easy enough.

"So, why are you on cooking duty, Grogen?" Mothy

asked as Wolflock's confidence began to increase.

"I didn't wanna be out there. The Cap'in won't come out of his cabin and the first mate is run over with problems. Normally, the Cap'in and him share it all, but now he's going under. Cap'in normally does the rosters and organisin', and Slavidus makes it happen. Now he 'as ta do it all by himself. Swamped cause the Cap'in is shut up. Only the first mate knows why and he ain't telling no one. And, on top o' that, all me plates are goin' missin'! People been keepin' em in their cabins when they ain't s'pose to."

"How long has that been going on for?" Wolflock asked, intrigued by the puzzle that the first mate was now a key piece to.

"'Bout two weeks now. I feel like I lose a plate a night," Grogen huffed.

"No, no. I knew that." Wolflock shook his head, although he was satisfied his deduction from earlier had been correct, "not the plates. The Captain."

"Just after we picked up our last few passengers at the crossing halfways between here and Corl," Grogen said. "I dunno how long Slavidus can keep this up, though. I give 'im til we hit the mountains before we 'ave to stop and figure it out."

"Who boarded two weeks ago?"

"I don't 'member. We've been so busy that I haven't been able to meet the new folk on board." Grogen stopped his stirring and thought for a while. "You'd 'ave to ask Slavidus, but he's so damn busy..."

Wolflock hummed as he thought. If they had to delay their journey, he wouldn't be able to enter Mystentine until Spring, which would mean he would have to go home in shame or find some kind of employment, as he doubted his father would be willing to send him an allowance. Neither option sounded pleasant.

But, if he could find out why the Captain was shut away, he could solve whatever the problem was to ensure their timely arrival and perhaps even receive deck privileges. He could also report back to Myna he'd made a good connection with an influential captain and possibly get something to send back home to Gruta before they left the country.

There were still more questions to ask and more data to acquire before he could draw any conclusions. Tiny threads of a mental web began to emerge. The state of the ship, the first mate keeping a secret of the captain's absence, the exhausted crew. All of it lit up in his mind like lamplight glinting off cobweb threads in an attic. The missing pieces were: what happened two weeks ago that could be so bad the captain would lock himself away and neglect the ship, and what would it take to reverse the situation.

He could see Mothy looking at him with curiosity, which surprised Wolflock. But, before he could explain anything, the passengers began flooding into the dining room.

"It ain't ready yet!" Grogen groaned and grabbed a sack of hemp seed bread. "Quick!" he growled, pouring the bread into Wolflock and Mothy's arms. "Pass these out and get the water and cups for 'em!"

"Aye, aye!" Mothy saluted with a loaf of the dark bread to his forehead.

He seemed to know where everything was, so Wolflock mirrored him on the other side of the room, which conveniently prevented them from running into one another with their jugs of water and wooden cups.

Soon, the dining room filled with light chatter and the smell of fresh soup, causing audible belly rumbles. Wolflock's legs began to ache from working for several hours, and he was so hungry that he could have eaten three bowls of the bland soup. Grogen used a ladle as big as Wolflock's head to scoop the soup into the wooden bowls, handing them to the boys to distribute the meals.

With two bowls in hand, Wolflock now had the excuse he needed to ask the passengers when they arrived and unearth any clues towards the Captain's isolation. First, he served the two dark-skinned ladies, acting as pleasant as possible.

"Merry meet, ladies!" He smiled with his teeth bared and placed the bowls down in front of them. "Having a nice trip, I hope?"

"Why, yes, thank you," said the taller one to his right, pulling away at the sight of his bumbling attempt at a smile. "Though, the trip was nicer when the Captain joined us. I'm glad to be gone soon."

"Enjoy your meal," he nodded and returned for two more bowls, eliminating two of the passengers from his list immediately.

Next he served the couple he had seen arguing earlier.

"Good evening," he said through his forced grin. "I trust your trip is going smoothly?"

The man looked up with a suspicious glare, but the lady returned his pleasantry. "Why, thank you. We haven't seen you on board before. I'm-"

The man started coughing loud enough to drown out her words, shooting a dangerous glare at her.

"I'm Wolflock. A pleasure to make your acquaintance. I got on at the Plugh dock. Where did you get on?"

"At Corl-" she started but was cut off again by the man's deliberate coughing.

"I hope the soup helps your illness." Wolflock's face dropped all civility, and he looked down his nose at the man's rudeness. But, even with the irritating encounter, Wolflock eliminated two more suspects. He was looking for someone who had gotten on at the last dock, judging by the two-week timeframe he'd been provided, which ruled out anyone who had boarded in Corl.

By the time Wolflock got the next two bowls, Mothy had already served the other half of the table and was starting at the opposite end from Wolflock, cutting the time he had to question the other passengers.

"Evening." He restored his polite smile for the man with the canvases and the beautiful woman he was animatedly talking to. "How is your trip going?"

"Exquisitely," purred the tanned man. Wolflock blinked as he saw he had one bright green eye and one brown eye. "Although, I truly wanted to do my work on the deck..." he finished with a dramatic sigh.

"Your work? I heard that being confined to our cabins was something to do with the Captain not emerging," Wolflock shrugged, trying to mimic the man's disappointment. He noted that although the man dressed modestly, his brown jacket was embroidered with dark yellow thread around the collar in a floral design. This told Wolflock he may not be wealthy, as the jacket was a simple wool, but he had artistic friends who had added the design after he had purchased the coat. He had pockets stitched in odd places, but the seams were crooked and showed through the other side of his coat. He was practical and not fussed about his own appearance.

"Veluse and I only saw him once when we boarded with Tanni and her daughter. I'm Yifi by the way. Merry meet." The lady's soft voice was tinged with a giggle from Veluse's dramatic behaviour.

Wolflock had never seen a woman with such perfect skin. Absolutely flawless, but not a trace of powder on her cheeks. She was also dressed modestly, with a high neck dress that hung loosely around her upper arms and draped over her frame in an attempt to hide her figure, but the fabrics were a much finer quality than her dinner companion. The Pyringel soft leather had to be worked over constantly for several days and would harden if it got wet, and the blend of cotton and silk made her dress shimmer slightly. It was clear she didn't want people paying any heed to her beauty.

"How will I ever pay the Captain if I cannot paint

his visage!?" he cried and swooped his hand to his head. "The stress is making me all clammy, and I fear I may fall ill!"

"I see... I'm Wolflock. A pleasure to meet you both." Wolflock struggled to maintain his smile in the face of Veluse's melodramatics. While the brown-haired Yifi calmed Veluse down by cajoling him with a soothing stroke of his arm, Wolflock looked around the room for Tanni and Tinni. Yifi had helped him narrow down who he should inquire after.

He dashed back to the kitchen area where Mothy had already collected the last two bowls.

"Oh! I'll take those. You've already done most of them. Let me serve the last two," Wolflock insisted, and scooped the bowls out of Mothy's hands.

"You must really want to meet your new subjects." Mothy surrendered the bowls and gathered two more for their own dinner. "I'll be waiting for you at the prince's seating!"

"Knock it off," Wolflock couldn't help but snicker.

He started to wonder in the back of his mind if he'd made a friend. Surely not. It couldn't have been that easy. Maybe it was just the people in Plugh who were difficult. Or Mothy was special. Or he wanted something. Perhaps he was lonely on the ship. Whatever the reason,

Wolflock knew he would discover it eventually.

He made his way back over to the table and saw the lady and child he'd met earlier eating their bread. They had been the last to come into dinner.

"Hello again!" Wolflock presented a more genuine smile to the pair, having already met them, and put their bowls down. He rubbed his aching arms, grateful to be done with all the climbing and manual labour for the day.

"Merry meet!" piped the young girl. "I'm Tinni!" She jumped up on her seat and stretched out her hand in an overt display of friendliness. Her mother didn't seem to pay any heed, lost in her own thoughts.

"An enormous pleasure to meet you, Tinni," Wolflock chuckled and shook her hand back with a mock formality. "How is your journey progressing?"

"Very, very well! I've made two friends now! Oh! Can I have some more food for later? I get hungry after dinner."

"How very lovely. I'll get you some seconds to take away. And, how are you, ma'am?" He touched the mother's shoulder. Her black dress was covered in a thick lace design with black dull beads from Pyringel. He could tell by the jagged diamond shapes and changing striations. She wasn't native to their though. Her complexion was too pale. This must have been an expensive trip for her to make by land and river. There was no indication of how she financed it.

"I will be fine once we get to Hatfjorn Lake..." She sighed and picked up her spoon, idly stirring her meal. "Thank you. We're fine now."

Wolflock understood the conversation was over, so he bowed to Tinni, who giggled at his display of formality, and joined Mothy at the very end of the table, sitting down to his meal with a groan of relief before he picked up his spoon.

"You don't strike me as the '*merry meet*' type. Why were you talking to everyone?" Mothy asked through a mouthful of vegetables.

Wolflock rolled his spoon in his long fingers as he contemplated whether or not to discuss his plan with his new acquaintance. He felt there was a level of comradery between them after their day together and although he was still a bit suspicious, he thought it would be a good test of Mothy's secret keeping abilities. Normally he would bounce his ideas off Myna if he thought she wouldn't interfere, but without her here, it was nice to have someone else to discuss with.

"Well, the Captain has been locked in his quarters since the last stop, right?" he said in a low tone.

"Aye..."

"So that means that whoever got on at the last stop has something to do with that. Now, I've discovered who I need to examine more closely so we can get the Captain out and about again. That way I can spend the rest of the trip on the deck," he finished, puffing his chest out and raising a triumphant spoonful of soup. It wasn't as bland as he thought it would.

"That is very clever," Mothy hummed, "but you could have just asked me. I've been on the ship since it started its journey. I know everyone here."

Wolflock choked for a second and scowled, realising his new friend may be equally more useful and obtuse than he first thought. "Thanks for telling me..."

"Why are you doing it, anyway?" Mothy asked with a sideways glance from his food.

"So, I can get out on the deck when I like. This journey will be horrendously boring if I'm imprisoned on the second level. I'd rather be free to do as I please. Also, if we don't arrive on time, we won't be admitted into the university until next semester and I can't stand the thought of facing all of Plugh in such an embarrassing state," Wolflock scoffed, as if it were obvious.

Mothy's mouth twisted as if he'd tasted something unpleasant, but he returned to his food with a shrug, making Wolflock wonder if he was just holding his tongue or if the idea was something his new acquaintance hadn't thought of and would come around to.

Dinner was soon finished, but no one moved to the door. Some passengers chatted away while others strolled about, admiring the decor. No one seemed in a hurry to return to their confinement.

"We used to spend the evenings dancing, and they'd get the instruments out. Sometimes the crew would get their cards out and we'd play a few rounds of Gypsy Farm..." Mothy sighed.

"That certainly sounds a bit more entertaining than going to bed right away. I'm not tired at all."

Slavidus came in right as Grogen was serving Tinni her requested seconds, and announced that there would be no music or dancing this evening as the instruments were packed away and would stay that way until his workload decreased. Apparently, crew members were required to supervise the passengers in these activities, and none could be spared.

There was a great whining and groaning at the news, but he would hear none of it, shooing everyone back to their cabins. Luckily, for Wolflock and Mothy, they were permitted to stay longer as Grogen explained that they had "offered" to help him clean up. They were both given half barrels and scrubbing brushes made from wood, glue, and the coarse fur of a riverbank creature they had never heard of called a maramuti.

"They compete for river space with us in the summer," Grogen explained as they scrubbed the bowls. "But, in winter, the waters get too cold and they stick to the shores. We'll see their colony in abouts a week."

"*You'll* see the colony. We'll all be in our rooms," Mothy moaned, unable to keep his cheeky smile off his face. "Alone. In the dark. With no entertainment. Unless, of course, you let us out..."

"Haha. Nice try kiddo! You've been learnin' too much from Veluse... We'll see, though. If you 'elp me, I'll 'elp you." He winked.

Grogen pulled out a half-dried leaf and some herb, rolled it and lit it off the coals under the cauldron. Then he smoked while he watched the boys finish their work.

Wolflock thought he was being lazy, but, as he observed, he noticed that Grogen looked almost as exhausted and weary as Slavidus. The skin on his face sagged from being overworked, and his muscles strained to keep him upright. The sweet-smelling smoke wafted around them and Wolflock's eyes began to ache with lethargy. He saw Mothy's eyes were doing the same.

They finished scrubbing the bowls and laid them out to dry, went to the edge of the deck and threw the dirty water overboard, and slumped off to bed.

"If you get into any more mischief let me know," Mothy yawned and leaned on the doorframe. "Can't have you getting into trouble without me."

Wolflock chuckled in agreement. It was much more fun to get into trouble with someone else. They both collapsed on their beds, allowing the lulling rock of the ship to carry them to their dreams.

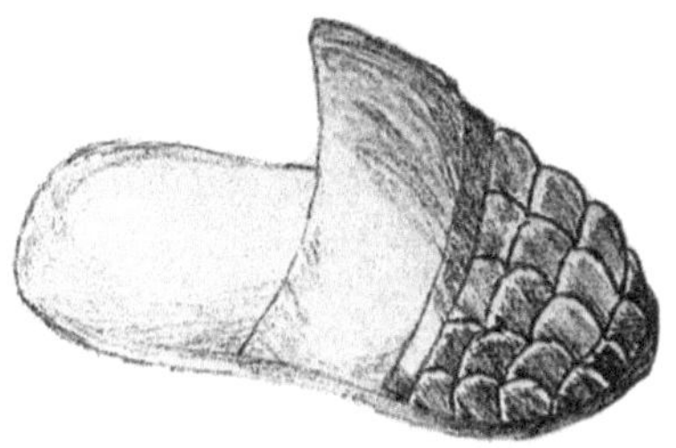

CHAPTER 8

The Silver Ice Hair-less

The next morning, Wolflock woke at dawn to the sounds of the creaking ship and the crew rushing around above deck. He could hear Slavidus' hoarse shout with the occasional crack in his voice from tiredness. He kept his eyes closed in the dim morning light, hoping to fall back asleep, but sleep had abandoned him.

Wolflock dragged himself up and pulled on his dark red quilted robe with matching slippers as he wondered if any of the crew had gotten more than three hours sleep. He combed his hair with his fine-toothed comb in the window's reflection until he felt presentable, but his face was still coated in a layer of the grime he'd soaked in from the kitchen. Looking around, he found there was no washing bowl or cloth to clean himself with.

He frowned. *They have forgotten to bring me one in this disorganised mess.*

He decided to go to Mothy's room and see if he had one. He knocked, but there was no answer. He waited a few more moments and knocked again louder. A grumpy cough echoed from the room over and he decided that instead of waking the whole ship, he would be better off nudging his new acquaintance awake. He opened the door and saw Mothy was in the single most awkward sleeping position he'd ever seen. He was belly down with one leg hanging out of the bed, one arm against the wall and the other bent over his head, snoring like someone sawing logs.

"Mothy?" Wolflock asked, and received a louder snore in response.

He rolled his eyes and walked to the stairs leading to the crew quarters, hoping to look for something more than a rag and bucket, but he wasn't hopeful. Going down the steep stairs at the end of the hall, he managed to find some dirty rags, but they were far from something he'd use to purify his face. The rest of the windowless hallway consisted of several hammocks, barrels, firewood and another set of stairs going down into the hull. He was on the verge of giving up forever on personal hygiene when he felt a strange breeze at his ankles.

The brisk sensation drew his eyes to the space underneath the stairs. He dropped down on all fours and saw a peculiar iron grate, wound into an intricate ship design, covering a large ventilation tunnel. Was it some kind of ventilation shaft? Or perhaps a smuggler's hiding hole? Unlike everything else on the ship, this grate was black iron, not silver or painted silver. It was intentionally meant to hide in the shadows, which made Wolflock want to look into it even more.

His curiosity ensnared him and, as he hadn't cleaned himself, he thought getting a little dirtier would do him no harm. Crawling under the wooden stairs, he looked through the dark grate and saw a beam of light shining down at the end. He glanced back, scoping the environment for onlookers. Seeing no one in their hammocks, Wolflock jiggled the grating and found it was attached with a hinge that lifted easily out of place.

The small tunnel was big enough for him to crawl through and, judging by the marks in the dust, someone else had been there within the last week. From the size and shape of the markings, it had to have been someone small. Possibly Mothy, but he couldn't be sure. There were also threads of long silver hair crammed into the corners, glinting in the light at the end of the crawl space.

He reached the end of the tunnel and found that the light was coming through an identical grate four feet above him, which lead into a bright room. He climbed up the rungs in the vent to the exit and opened it as quietly as he could.

Like the secret stairs that Mothy had shown him, this grate opened up under a table. It was much smaller and round, shrouded with a long white cloth trimmed with silver. He listened for a few moments, hoping to deduce where on the ship he now found himself. There were no crew noises. No passengers snoring. No clatter of pots and pans. All he could hear was someone sniffling several feet away and the faint, oaky smell of a man's perfume. He peeked out from under the tablecloth and glimpsed a large man with an extravagantly high collar, his head down on a desk and a Captain's broad black and silver hat beside him.

Wolflock crawled out from under the table, covered in cobwebs and dust, and studied the sobbing Captain. Realisation swept over him. This was it! He could speak to the man himself and find out what had kept him locked in here. He didn't look unwell besides his morose mood. Had someone died?

Wolflock quickly dusted as much of the tunnel dirt off his arms and legs as he could before he stood up straight and put one hand behind his back, wishing to give the most powerful man on board the best impression possible.

"Excuse me?" He coughed.

The Captain jumped up, his eyes red from crying and his head as bald as a pearl.

"AHHH!" he shouted and shielded his head with his arm. "Don't look at me! What are you doing in here?"

Wolflock jumped back into the table in shock. "I came to find out why you're unwell! There's nothing wrong with you!" he stammered, gawking at the man's shiny bald head.

"Nothing wrong? Nothing *wrong*?" The hysterical Captain clutched at his scalp as he advanced on Wolflock. "Can't you see it? Are you blind?"

"N-no, sir?" The Captain's manic behaviour bewildered Wolflock.

"This is the Silver Ice *Hair*! The Ice *Hair*!" he cried and began pacing, his long coat billowing behind him.

"And you're bald?"

The captain tried to keep his face steady, but his lip trembled and his eyes welled up with tears. "Nooooo!" he wailed and threw himself back on his desk. "Why did you go? Where did you go? Aujin! Oh, my Aujin!"

Wolflock's mind whirled as the puzzle began to take shape in his mind. His faint spider web caught just the right ray of light that illuminated the strands. The Captain had lost a sentient being that acted as his hair. Most likely a pet. That's why he was distraught, and that was why he hadn't been managing the ship.

There was just one thread he couldn't quite see clearly yet. He approached the Captain much as he would have approached a beached shark, speaking ever so softly, "Who is Aujin?"

"M-my sn-snuffle!" The Captain sobbed and blew his nose like a small trumpet into a handkerchief by his sleeve.

It made sense and Wolflock understood what was wrong. A snuffle was an animal that was native to the Syongdelen forest and resembled a long, thick ponytail with thin slit-like eyes and a soft mouth strong enough only to crunch bugs. The Captain was bald, yet his ship was called the *Silver Ice Hair*, which meant that the Captain used the pet snuffle as his false hair. A perfect disguise to continue the name and image of the ship. Furthermore, it was most likely a rare silver snuffle, given the name of the ship and the long hairs Wolflock found in the vent. The Captain's ego was no doubt wounded by the loss of his facade, and he was too embarrassed to show his hairless head to any of his crew or passengers. It was also evident that only the first mate knew the truth, but had been sworn to secrecy, and the stress was taking its toll on the entire ship.

"It's rather selfish of you to let your ship fall apart simply because your pet is missing," Wolflock scoffed. He had expected much more of such a prestigious captain. He'd been researching the Silver Ice Hair, its history and its captains for months and this was beneath his expectations. They were meant to be noble, proud pioneers for nautical travel. Not blubbering fools with image issues. "Just don a wig and be done with it."

"What?" Captain Blutro blinked. "That's not it, at all! Aujin has been with me for decades. He was the last gift my grandfather ever gave me. He's more than some mere pet! He's part of my very being!"

The captain's voice began to raise as Wolflock verbally prodded him and his anger dispersed the tears.

"Well, *Captain*," Wolflock snarled, "while you're moping in here your ship, which if I'm not mistaken, was given to you by your father and grandmother, is falling apart because it has no leader!"

"What are you talking about? Slavidus is-"

"Not equipped to do the job of two people. Now

bald or not, your ship needs you."

Captain Blutro's face cracked with pain. "I can't. My crew believe in me and if they find out I've been deceiving them, they'll never trust my judgement again. They'll think the journey is cursed and jump ship at the Kreiger Zwerg dock."

"Meaning we'd be stranded regardless? Surely they'd be understanding of the situation."

The captain shook his shiny head. "Ship folk are highly superstitious. This would dismantle the crew. That's why Slavidus is the only person on board charged with my secret."

Wolflock scrunched his nose as he thought, finally having to pinch the bridge of it to control his thoughts from wanting him to bully the captain into letting him run the ship. It couldn't be that hard. He had a fair clue about what the ropes around the vessel did now.

No. Don't do that. You won't have any time to relax and enjoy the journey.

"What can you tell me about Aujin and his disappearance?"

The captain took a breath as he recalled whatever he could through the period of emotional distress. "It was two weeks ago. Just after the crossing at Corl. We took on four new passengers and three departed. Everything was fine and I finished my shift, Slavidus took over and I put myself and Aujin to bed. When I woke up he was gone. Not a trace of him anywhere. The room was locked, the doors to the balcony and the windows were all locked to keep the cold out. Slavidus searched the ship for me, but Aujin is nowhere to be found. I was so anxious when we stopped at Seebrueke. What if he was smuggled off the ship? What if I've lost him and my crew forever?" The captain started to weep again into his sleeve.

Wolflock squinted, looking for other clues around the room. The only obvious way out was the grate under the central table, and judging by the hairs in there, the snuffle had been able to slip through the holes easily. Someone else had been in there, though. What would have drawn the snuffle in there? And who would want to steal it?

"Has he ever gone missing before?" Wolflock asked. He thought about Brennan and how susceptible he was to being lead with apples. "Would he be lured away by food?"

"Ever since he was a kit he's been very fussy about his food. He's only ever run off once, fifteen years back when lived on scraps from the kitchen. He was as sick as a mermaid eating bread!"

"I... don't have a reference for what that looks like." Wolflock pulled a face as he tried to picture a slender dolphin-like woman going green.

"It ain't pretty. But that was only a week. This has been a whole fortnight! He's probably damn near death now! Oh, my poor baby... And I couldn't save him because of my arrogance! What have I done?" he wailed into his hands as he fell back into his chair.

"When I get it back for you, will you let me out on the deck whenever I please?"

"W-what?" He looked up, blinking his tears away.

"And a washing bowl with fresh towels every morning."

"S-sure?"

"And I would like writing implements."

"Anything you like if you can get Aujin back to me."

Wolflock nodded once and to avoid the first mate he could hear yelling at one of the crewmen just outside in the passenger hallway, he climbed under the table and down the grate, leaving the Captain stupefied at his mysterious exit.

He crawled back through the grate and hid under the stairs until the coat was clear of crewmates carrying up supplies for meals, and dashed back to Mothy's room, already devising how he'd find out who was responsible for the missing snuffle. Only four people had gotten on between Plugh and Corl. Veluse, the dramatic artist, Yifi, the lovely lady, Tanni, the widow, and Tinni, her daughter.

They were his prime suspects, and he decided the best course of action would be to systematically go through their possible motives for taking the Captain's snuffle. But, first, he needed some help.

He burst into Mothy's room and strode up to him, still asleep, and flicked his ear.

The response was phenomenal.

Mothy jumped to the side, hit the wall, slipped off the bed, grunted, coughed, farted, and pulled all the bedding off with him.

"Huh?" He looked up groggily, rubbing his head. "What was that for?"

"I need to know about some of the passengers! Quick!" Wolflock demanded and hoisted him to his feet.

"I need food first... and you've got a spider in your hair. Nice slippers. Have you been sleepwalking?"

He explained the situation as Mothy got dressed and they moved to Wolflock's room for him to get changed before putting the spider on the deck. As the crew and company readied for breakfast, the passengers made their way incrementally to the dining hall, relishing the sunlight and fresh air.

He finished his tale before they entered the dining hall, greeted by the sweet perfume of dates and spiced porridge. The boys collected their breakfast and Wolflock inhaled his to have it out of the way while Mothy ate at a far more relaxed pace, speaking between mouthfuls.

"Goodness! How ironic that the captain is bald," he chuckled. "So, who did you want to know about? I don't think anyone would have stolen it. They're all good people."

"Until proven otherwise, they are all just *people* to me. Let's start with Tanni and her daughter," Wolflock said, leaning forward and keeping his voice low.

"You didn't have many friends back home, did you, my prince? Must have been lonely in your castle tower." Mothy gave him a mocking look of pity. "Tanni said to me when she first boarded that she's going to Hatfjorn Lake to live with her parents. Her husband died on his brother's farm between Chaysaile and Wathers. They were deeply in love and wealth wasn't an issue, but, now that he's dead, his brother gets the whole estate because she didn't want to manage it. She said the memories upset her too much.

"She's got enough supplies to get home, and the

knowledge to set up a store, but she will have to work hard to raise a child and care for her ageing parents. She'd been married for eight years, so I think she's nearly thirty. Tinni is four. She's a happy child and I don't think she understands the whole thing with her father... she doesn't seem bothered by much." There was definitely financial motive for Tanni, but it was odd for Tinni to be oblivious to her mother's grief as well. Children were like uncomfortable sponges for surrounding emotions as far as Wolflock was concerned. He didn't let Mothy have another mouthful before he continued questioning him.

"What about Veluse?"

"Oh, him!" Mothy smiled and rolled his eyes. "He's fun. Very eccentric, and he's been wanting to paint a portrait of the Captain on the deck so he can relax for the rest of the trip. That's how he's paying. He's travelling to Hatfjorn Lake to paint the landscape and the mountains, and see what other things he can gain inspiration from."

Wolflock imagined him using the snuffle as inspiration as they were quite unique, or even using it to make paint brushes from their treasured hair. Perhaps there were other artistic qualities a silver snuffle may hold that he wasn't aware of. He would have to find some specific means of gaining the necessary information from Veluse without tipping him off.

"And Yifi?"

"She is very quiet and smart. Nice looking, too. She's going to Mystentine to see one of her childhood friends. She came from Shellinden, but moved to Corl to get away from a poor engagement. She told me she's had more than fifty marriage proposals! I think she's been hurt in the past by superficial men, and now she's travelling to find a life partner who sees beyond her appearance. Veluse has already painted a portrait of her. He gets to paint all kinds of ladies. He gave me a quick peek in his sketchbook, and you wouldn't believe the different shapes they can take! Like this one who looked like her pug dog from Corl-"

Wolflock had stopped listening to Mothy as his mind wandered onto the most beautiful lady on board. It was possible that Yifi could use the silver snuffle to disguise herself as a crone to keep away the onslaught of suitors as she searched for people who were more attracted to her personality.

Wolflock's theories developed, linking the four people to the missing snuffle in his mental spider web. Tanni could want to use the rare silver snuffle to gain more wealth so she could live comfortably, or Tinni may be keeping it as a pet of some kind.

Before he could continue his train of thought, Yifi

came into the dining room and looked furtively around as she made her way to get some of the bubbling porridge. They watched her as she continued to flick her eyes back to the door.

Wolflock looked at Mothy's curious expression and deduced that this was not normal behaviour for Yifi. He scrutinised her features. Her dark hair sat in long, voluptuous bundles around her head in the Chaysaile fashion. Her dress was simple and plain, but that couldn't mask her beautiful, voluptuous figure. She had a soft, rounded form that denoted wealth and fertility. In most parts of Puinteyle, she would have been highly sought after as a romantic partner.

The door banged open, and the first mate stormed through, glaring about as if he'd lost something. Wolflock gave him a double glance as he watched Yifi hide herself behind the table, pretending to have dropped her cutlery. Slavidus huffed and stormed out before anyone could speak to him.

"What was that about?" Mothy asked as he finished the rest of his food.

"I do not know... But I will certainly find out. Now, where did Yifi-"

They both looked at the door as it shut, and caught a brief flash of her dress as she fled from the dining room.

Wolflock rose and strode from the table, followed by Mothy who wiped his mouth on his sleeve.

"So, no seconds for you then?" Mothy asked with his usual smile.

"Not hungry for food." Wolflock's brow furrowed. His mind was set on the puzzle at hand.

CHAPTER 9
Yifi's Curse

They left the dining hall and saw Yifi rush downstairs to the cabins, but, before she got more than halfway, she whirled around and rushed back up the stairs and hid behind several barrels.

Their confused stares caught her gaze as she peeked over the rim. She silently pleaded with them by pressing her finger to her lips. They soon saw why when the first mate emerged from the lower deck with his hands balled into fists and his mouth twisted in a furious snarl.

"Boys!" he snapped. His hair was even less tidy than

the day before and the bags under his eyes had grown darker from his lack of sleep. "Have you seen Yifi?"

"No? Why?" Wolflock said with a cool stare over his shoulder, gazing away from the short tempered Slavidus and towards Yifi's hiding spot. Mothy followed his lead and scratched his chin as if he were thinking.

"Uh... No particular reason," he stammered, and coughed as his face flushed red. Wolflock noted his change in demeanour. It was evident Slavidus was not used to being questioned or refused and disrupted his emotional state. Wolflock could relate. "Just something that the Captain wanted. She took something... Official kind of business, you understand. I meant to talk to her about it yesterday, but she's never without company. It's a delicate matter."

"Where haven't you looked?" Mothy asked as he scratched the back of his neck, glancing to the ground to avoid Slavidus' piercing glare.

"Unless she jumped overboard, then she would be in the hull, but none of the passengers are allowed down there, and the only reason someone would go down there is to hide. Perhaps she snuck out on deck..." Slavidus mumbled to himself as he brushed past them and walked towards the helm.

Once he was out of earshot, Wolflock leaned

against the barrels, pretending to bask in the sunshine. They could see the crew were busy with their duties, and he knew it would only be a few moments before they were told to move back to their cabins.

"Oh, thank you!" Yifi sighed, staying hidden behind the barrels.

"You'd be more welcome if you told us why he was really after you? What official Captain business was he talking about?" Wolflock pressed and cast a discerning eye around to make sure that no one else could hear. Perhaps Slavidus' own investigation had led him to Yifi since they left Seebruecke.

"I... ah.... umm " she twisted her hands, "well.. "

"Out with it. Now," Wolflock demanded, uncaring of how affronted she was by his manner.

He assumed that she was used to people doting on her, giving her everything she desired and more, even if she wasn't inclined to reciprocate the act.

Wolflock was well aware of the benefits of being aesthetically pleasing. He was rather handsome, himself, and, during his younger years, he'd used that to persuade staff and teachers to do favours for him that they would not have otherwise done. It never lasted long, but he could always rely on one or two instances where he would receive special privileges. He'd had teachers lend him books that other students hadn't been privy to, and many of the shop owners had gone above and beyond to cater to his often flippant desires for the introductory phase of their acquaintance.

As such, he was well aware of the power that Yifi had at her disposal. She was a spectacularly beautiful woman, and she seemed to glow with a powerful aura that attracted grown men and women with unnatural ease. However, Wolflock, delighted in believing he was an exception, remained unmoved by her physical appearance. For him, it was merely something to observe rather than to covet. In fact, Wolflock had never desired a man or woman based on their look. before. So, he had calculated that his manner may shock Yifi into revealing what he wanted.

"Slavidus said you took something from the Captain," Mothy leant back on the barrels as well, lifting his face up to take in the warm sunlight. "Is it true Yifi? You don't strike me as a thief."

"That's because I am not one!" Yifi snapped. "I took nothing from the Captain at all! I have not seen the Captain since I first boarded this ship. If he would come out, he may finally stop Slavidus from his relentless pursuit of me!"

Mothy stared, taken aback by her vehement

outburst, but Wolflock's eyes narrowed as he focused on the clues she had revealed.

"Ahah! I knew that was the reason you had been sneaking around!" Wolflock smiled in triumph.

"For your information I *always* sneak around. I do it because of this curse on my face. At birth I was cursed by my insane, disfigured mother to make me so attractive that men and women could not resist me. Most men, and many women, can't keep themselves from me, but I refuse to be passed around and have my heart trampled again. Yes, I'm sneaking around, but I have a good reason. I refuse to allow someone to love me purely because of my appearance. I need a real love of the heart and mind, not the body." She sighed, sadness colouring her expression.

"When I first arrived, Slavidus was gentlemanly, and I thought he might be different. I gave him a little affection, and we talked whenever he was free, but then the Captain kept to his room, and, the wearier Slavidus got, the more beastly he became!" She finished by crossing her arms and facing away from them, but Wolflock noted a hint of dejection in her countenance.

"And you enjoy Veluse's company because he prefers men, yes?"

"Veluse prefers male company in a romantic

manner, yes." Yifi nodded, relaxing. "That makes him less inclined to act like a buffoon around me."

"How on earth did you know that Veluse preferred men!?" Mothy's jaw dropped. "He told me of all the women he's seen naked and-"

"*Seen*, Mothy. *Seen.*"

"I don't follow..." Mothy put his hand behind his head and smiled in embarrassment.

"He's a painter, an artist," Wolflock explained. "He would know how beautiful women understand their bodies to be. And many women like to have themselves painted nude to preserve the image of their physical beauty, but Veluse only sees them naked. He cares a great deal about his craft. I saw that his canvases were cared for quite well, tied with a delicate fabric used to keep plants unbruised. He was also the only man of age that I've seen Yifi interacting with, which would lead one to conclude that he does not fancy her, and she would feel comfortable around him because he would not make any unwanted advances unto her."

"Brilliant!" Mothy grinned and shook his head in amazement. "Next, you'll be telling better fortunes than the twins!"

"Do we have mystics on board the ship? Regardless, that doesn't explain why we originally wanted to speak to Yifi," he said, dancing around discussing the Captain's hair.

Yifi and Mothy stayed silent while Wolflock closed his eyes and frowned, deep in thought. It was a habit for Wolflock to think over all the possibilities, mapping out every detail in his mind as he went through his mental plan of the ship, plank by plank thinking of where the Captain's snuffle was and who could have taken it.

He had to tackle the next suspect on his list. He didn't have enough knowledge of Veluse to just go bursting into his room, but Yifi did. He could use her as a way to snoop around his room and find evidence of Aujin being there, or get the artist to incriminate Yifi and turn the attention back onto her. Either way, the next logical step to revealing more of his mental web laid with Veluse.

Yifi and Mothy walked with him into the dining room without him noticing and they had another bowl of porridge as an excuse to stay out of the cabins for longer while he developed his plan.

"We'll have to speak to Veluse. I have to rule something out. He wasn't at breakfast today. He's feeling unwell, isn't he?"

"I'm not sure. I was trying to hide all morning."

"Mothy, go and get some tea for him."

Mothy stopped with a spoon halfway to his mouth, raised an eyebrow and placed the spoon down again, folding his arms and leaning back against his chair.

"Sorry, your majesty, but I don't do anything without a display of proper manners. I hereby dub myself your etiquette instructor because clearly you need one."

Wolflock sighed out of his nose, rolling his eyes at Mothy before he pinched the bridge of his nose. "I don't know how to make tea! Just do it." Mothy turned his face away with his nose pointedly in the air as he pretended to not hear Wolflock. "... Please."

"Of course I will." Mothy pushed his chair out and swivelled around, leaping to his feet. "Anything to make Veluse feel better."

Wolflock frowned. It annoyed him that submission was tantamount to manners with his new friend. "Come with me, Yifi. If you stay downstairs with Mothy, Veluse and I, Slavidus is less likely to ambush you."

She nodded and linked arms with him as they descended the stairs. Her olive skin was soft, and she smelled like fresh honey. Wolflock felt a tinge of guilt about being so harsh with her earlier, but he didn't deem it severe enough to merit an apology.

The first thing he noticed when they entered

Veluse's room was that it smelt like paint and perfume. Just as Wolflock had predicted, the artist lay in his bed sweating, all the colour drained from his face.

"Ah..." he croaked, "Yifi... you've come to see my end. Such an angel..."

"Oh, my sweet friend. You're not dying. It's just a cold." She smiled and brought his hand to her cheek. "You've got a chill. Mothy is being a dear and bringing you some tea."

Wolflock began looking about the room, but all the paint brushes were made of normal fibres, such as horsehair and other fine furred creatures. None of which were silver. There wasn't even a silver strand to be found on his bedding. Wolflock sighed, turning to sit on the bed and wait for Mothy to arrive, but, as he did, he saw something twinkling under the bed. Had Veluse killed the snuffle? It wasn't moving...

Wolflock picked up a paintbrush and sat on the bed next to Yifi, fiddling with it for a moment before he pretended to drop it and kick it under the bed.

"Whoops. Let me just get that!" He ducked down, chest to the ground, to grab the brush and inspect whatever glittered beneath the bed.

Unfortunately, the silver strands were only the tassels along the edge of a folded shawl. Veluse had put a few items under his bed, such as his shoes and a jewellery box, but he had wrapped the shawl around a small canvas. Wolflock couldn't help himself. He lifted the shawl and peeked under it. He had painted all the male crew members in a group portrait with no clothes on and in suggestive positions, tastefully obscuring their genitals. It was a magnificent painting, but Wolflock wasn't prepared for that image and banged his head on the bottom of the bed as he scrambled out.

"Ouch."

"Veluse! I have tea for you! Miss Nü said this would help your cold."

Mothy rushed in and nearly spilt the tea as he skipped around Wolflock on the floor.

"Oh, my friends..." Veluse croaked, sitting up to accept the tea. "Thank you so much. My spirit is as warm as this drink now."

Wolflock flashed a polite smile as he stood up and caught Mothy's arm before he got too comfortable. "I think I'd like some tea as well."

"Ah! For that, your majesty, you'll need to learn how to do it yourself."

"Well... uh... come and teach me, then."

Mothy's eyes narrowed in suspicion, but he maintained his smile.

"It would be my pleasure. We'll be back later, Veluse. Look after him, Yifi. You're the best company he could ask for."

They dodged Slavidus on their way back to the dining hall so he couldn't send them back to their rooms. Once back in the kitchen area, Mothy brewed tea for them.

"Did you find something out about Veluse? Now you put the tea in the pot as it boils. Mama used to say 'for medicine a gentle simmer, for the morning a firm boil'..."

This was something Wolflock could do well. He had a steady hand and a proclivity for brewing various potions and science experiments. "He's not the person we're looking for. He's just a... ahem... good artist."

"Well, that rules out Yifi and Veluse. But I don't think Tanni or Tinni would steal anything. They're so sweet and well natured. Make sure you pour it at an angle so only a few leaves leak through... and we're done! Perfect tea. Honey?"

Wolflock gripped his chin in thought. "You need to remove emotional attachment in lieu of facts and proof. Their motivations don't seem particularly strong for this crime... unless..."

Wolflock paused for a long time, thinking things

through. Yifi had been hiding from Slavidus since the captain locked himself away and relinquishing the snuffle would have been the easy way out of that situation. Even using it to blackmailing Slavidus and the captain to leave her be was a plausible option. It couldn't be her. No evidence from Veluse's room proved he was the culprit either.

There was one element that he hadn't yet voiced that seemed to tie everything together.

"Tinni," he whispered to himself.

A shrill cry shattered his thoughts, and Tanni threw open the dining room doors, frantically scouring the room.

"Tinni? Tinni, where are you?"

CHAPTER 10

Hidden Hair

"Tinni? Tinni, are you in here? This is *not* funny, Tinni!"

Tanni's outburst startled the entire room. She flung herself at the nearest end of the table, seizing the white fabric and tearing it away. Oblivious to the stares and gasps of onlookers, she sent dinnerware crashing to the ground. Tanni then dropped to her knees to search under the table.

Wolflock and Mothy rose together and approached her, eyeing each other. Wolflock frowned with concern. Her anxiety was palpable. He placed a hand on her trembling shoulder. She jumped up from under the table, eyes widening in recognition. Wolflock winced as she gripped his upper arms like a vice.

"Wolflock! Oh, thank goodness! You know where Tinni is right?"

Wolflock shook his head and Tanni's frantic eyes welled with tears.

"Oh, my Tinni! I can't bear the thought of losing you, too!" She fell to her knees, sobbing into her hands with heaving gasps.

"Tanni, take a breath," Mothy soothed as he knelt down to hug her. "We'll find her. She can't have gone far."

"What if she fell overboard!" Tanni wrenched her face free of her hands and tore at her hair.

"Doubtful... The crow's nest is occupied constantly, and Tinni appears to be quite social, so she wouldn't have strayed out of sight." Wolflock's mind locked into finding the child as he rose to his feet. There were only a few places on the ship that weren't frequented by crew and company. One in particular that was the natural decision when trying to hide something taken from the captain's stateroom. "I believe I know where she is. You must wait here though. I'll bring her to you. Mothy, look after her."

"I shall do my duty, your majesty." Mothy saluted him with a spoon.

Tanni was deaf to everything around her, wailing in despair as Wolflock dashed from the room.

He ran down the stairs to the passenger deck, vaulted down to the crew deck and raced down the steep stairs to the hull, looking around the dark creaking space with wide eyes.

He wanted to kick himself for not realising it sooner. *The dust marks in the vent coupled with the silver hair. Aujin was a regular inhabitant of that vent and someone new had been in it recently. The bag she had been talking into when he first saw her. She was unaffected by the grief of her father. The best hiding spot on the ship, Slavidus had said. Grogen's plates going missing.*

"Shh, Slinky! They'll find us and mama won't let me have you as a pet," he heard an urgent whisper in the distance.

"Tinni?" he called out and climbed over the crates as he headed towards the noise. As he drew nearer, he caught the dim light of a lantern. Tinni was hiding in the dark, covering something behind her back. Empty plates, a blanket, a hairbrush, and a small fairy dust lantern surrounded her.

"What have you got there, little Miss?" he asked softly, and knelt down to be at eye level with her.

"Nothing..." she lied, diverting her gaze to the

ground.

"He isn't yours, is he? How did you keep him down here?" Wolflock asked, curious about why such a loyal pet hadn't already returned to its master.

"I found Slinky on the ship... I just kept feeding him and brushing him and he stayed. He eats my vegetables." Her lip trembled and her eyes welled with tears.

"It's ok, Tinni. You won't get in trouble. But we need to give him back now, aye?"

"Who does he belong to?"

"He's actually the Captain's. He's going to be so happy to see you have kept him safe. Can I see him?" He reached out with a gentle smile.

Tinni nodded, wiped her eyes with the sleeve of her dress and stepped to the side to reveal a beautiful, two-foot-long snuffle that was glimmering in the lantern light with silky silver hair. The long strands of hair hid its eyes, and it made a little sniffling noise as it snaked towards them. It certainly didn't look like it was on the verge of death. In fact... Wolflock thought it looked a little fat.

"It's ok, Slinky." Tinni beckoned the creature forward to Wolflock. "He's a friend."

Wolflock blinked in alarm when he heard a whistling grunt from the snuffle that sounded like it had mimicked Tinni as she said "friend".

The snuffle retreated around Tinni's ankle and she gave him a light brush with her tiny hand, giggling as he snuggled into her.

"Watch!" Tinni smiled and picked up a small canvas ball. "He does tricks too."

She threw the ball for the snuffle who slithered away in the dim light and nosed the ball back to her. They repeated the game a few times to show off for Wolflock.

In that moment Wolflock felt a growing awareness that if he said the wrong thing now Tinni's adventurous spirit would be crushed, and it was likely that the grief of her father would weigh on her as it had her mother. He didn't know why, but he had an urge to be kind to this child. She had been friendly to him and he wouldn't gain anything by upsetting her. He could do this and make sure all parties were happy.

He had to keep the Captain's secret from the others though. How could he get a child to keep it, too? It would be a gamble, but he had to try.

"Everyone on the ship is going to be so happy when Slinky is given back to the Captain. You'll be the secret heroine. Speaking of secrets, since you took such good care of this snuffle, I'm going to share something with you that makes us extra special passengers, aye?"

Tinni's eyes widened with excitement. She followed

Wolflock to the second level as he led her behind the stairs to the opposite end of the crew deck, where he pulled open the iron grate he had found that morning. He climbed in first, waving for them to follow. Tinni didn't need to crawl, she just ducked her head, and the silver snuffle followed her eagerly.

Wolflock pushed open the other iron grate, hoisting himself out under the Captain's table. Wolflock gave a polite nod to the Captain who looked just as bewildered as when he'd left him. He reached down into the vent to help Tinni out, chuckling as the Captain's eyes went as wide as saucers. He rose with a dumbfounded gasp as their final companion wriggled out around Tinni's ankle.

"Aujin!" he cried and rushed forward, grabbing the snuffle and hugging it close to his chest. Joy overwhelmed him as he cradled the snuffle like a baby. "You're alive! You've come back! I thought I'd never see you again! Oh, my light!"

Tinni giggled at the Captain's antics, laughing louder still when he turned his affection onto Wolflock, embracing him in a tight bear-like hug. The snuffle being returned meant more than the Captain's pride being restored, and Wolflock could see the full effect as the captain's tears of happiness slowly evaporated and his voice grew stronger.

"My boy! My boy! You've done it! You astounding, wonderful, lad!"

"Th-thanks," he coughed, winded by the burly embrace. "It was Tinni who found him for me, though."

"And, you, little one! Did you look after my Aujin while he was away?" His voice was booming with gratitude towards Tinni, who nodded shyly at the sudden attention.

"Yes, Captain Blutro."

"How on earth... but he's grown huge! How did you get him to eat?"

Tinni rocked back and forth on her heels. "He likes my vegetables."

Captain Blutro stopped for a moment, blinking in astonishment, then boomed with laughter.

"Bravo! Bravo, little one! Well, I'm so glad he's home! Vegetables instead of insects for you from now on, Aujin!" He beamed and raised the snuffle to his shoulder.

Right away the snuffle snuggled into his neck and slithered to the top of his head, biting down and producing what looked like a long ponytail that stemmed from the apex of his scalp.

"Can I come and see him sometimes?" Tinni asked, clinging onto Wolflock's trousers.

"You and Mr Wolflock are very welcome to come and see me any time after tea. As long as we keep little

Aujin our secret. But, right now, I need to run a ship!" He charged out of his room, flinging open his door as he crammed his hat on and went to take control of his vessel once more.

Wolflock smiled at the changed man and looked down at Tinni. "We can only talk about this to each other and the Captain, aye? Do I have your promise on that?"

Tinni nodded again and released his trousers to take his hand.

"Very good. Now, your mother is very worried about you, little Miss. Let's go and let her know you haven't fallen overboard. But, we need to keep this adventure our little secret... what are you going to tell your mother?"

"I made a friend called Slinky and played with them in the hull!" She smiled, baby teeth on full display.

"Can we say your friend was imaginary?" he offered as a compromise.

"My imaginary friend, Slinky. Um... yes!"

"And the real Slinky is our secret, yes?"

She nodded and sealed her lips as if she was locking a door with a key. Together, they strode out into what felt like a brand-new ship.

CHAPTER 11

New Growth

Wolflock and Tinni climbed to the top deck and beheld a miraculous scene. The Captain had clapped the astonished first mate on the shoulder and told him his shift was over. They both giggled at how Slavidus nearly burst into tears of joy when the Captain walked past him to the helm, immediately starting to organise the ramshackle crew. With the captain's happiness spreading through the ship like wildfire, the whole vessel seemed illuminated with a silver glow. It was as if the ship itself had returned to life.

It only took them a few minutes to find Mothy and Tanni, still waiting in the dining room. Mothy had made Tanni several cups of tea, but, the moment Tanni saw her daughter, she lunged forward, splintering the cup as she flung it away and rushed to hold the child tightly to her chest.

"Oh, my darling! My daughter! Thank you, Wolflock! Thank you!" Tanni sobbed with joy as Tinni struggled to escape her mother's clutches. "Wherever was she?!"

"Mama, I wasn't gone long! I was just playing."

"She was just playing with her imaginary friend in the hull." He shrugged with a smile, winking when he caught Mothy's eye. "I think the Captain is allowing us on the deck now." He jerked his head to the door, gesturing to Mothy that he'd answer his unasked questions out of earshot.

"Really? I mean- I didn't doubt you for a moment, my prince," Mothy grinned as he matched Wolflock's stride.

Wolflock gave Mothy a side glare for the royalty remark, but he couldn't help but smile. He felt excited to tell Mothy everything that had just happened.

They left Tanni fawning over Tinni in the dining room and entered the sunlight of the deck, taking in the fresh smell and spray of the river, making their way to the front of the deck where Wolflock felt they could talk in private.

The crew stood around as the Captain announced his apology to them all for falling so suddenly ill, but now that he was returned, everyone was to get extra rations and an extra week off in Creast when they reached their final port. The relief that washed over the ship was extraordinary. The crew, although still weary, smiled and relaxed, and the first point of call was to clear the top deck of all storage so the passengers could enjoy the day.

"How on earth did you know where she was? And how did you get the Captain out? I thought his pet would have been dead from what you told me earlier," Mothy asked, bewildered.

Wolflock took a deep breath of clean, fresh air. "The Captain mysteriously began hiding away after the last group of people came on board, so one of them had to have a connection to the problem, as it would have been highly unlikely that the two events would be unrelated. Then, when I went looking for a washcloth, I found a passage into the Captain's chambers by accident and found out that..." He stopped and looked around for anyone who may be listening, then beckoned for Mothy to lean closer, "...he's bald."

Mothy nodded eagerly. "Yes... I already understood that part of it. But he had-"

Wolflock shushed him, lowering his voice as he continued. "He has a snuffle. It went missing and his pride was too wounded to cope with people finding out about the ruse of his defining silver hair. Apparently, it ran the risk of damaging their trust in such a way that they would desert the ship at the very next dock. Also, as a lifelong companion, he was heartbroken at the thought that it was dying somewhere aboard his vessel or smuggled away forever."

Mothy nodded in understanding, "That sounds right. The crew are a loyal bunch, but if they found out the captain had tricked them they'd start wondering what else he had lied to them about."

Wolflock continued, even though he thought the unforgiving nature of something so fickle to be ridiculous. "I offered to get it back for him, as I knew that he would be unable to leave his room and Slavidus would be too busy managing the ship to search. I still believed it to still be on the ship, but finding it with all due haste was essential, for the ship would have been delayed far too long had it stayed missing, or had it been found deceased. I'm sure the captain would have stopped the ship entirely if that were the case.

"From what I'd read about them, snuffles are normally loyal and won't stray too far from those that feed them, which left me thinking that whoever had it was definitely looking after it, for the creature to be gone for so long. That's why I asked you about the other passengers.

"I also remembered seeing Tinni talking into a bag when I first boarded, then, later, I saw markings in the dust of that vent I mentioned, showing someone fairly small had gone in there recently. There were also long silver hairs indicating that the snuffle and child could have met there.

"After eliminating Veluse and Yifi as suspects, the

evidence all lead to Tinni, rather than Tanni, who has been rather inactive during her time on board. Tinni was keeping it in the hull with food and daily care. When her mother said she was missing on the ship, it also confirmed for me that Tinni was likely the one hiding the snuffle. The only place people go so rarely that they could have missed it is in the hull, and, as Slavidus mentioned earlier, it was one of the best hiding places on the ship. The rest of the ship had been thoroughly searched, no doubt, by her distraught mother. So logically, the only place left for her to hide was amongst the storage boxes in the hull. And, now that all is right and well, we have a happy Captain, deck privileges and this lovely weather!" He finished his conclusions in satisfaction and leaned against the railing.

"Marvellous! Positively marvellous! What a fabulous brain you have, my prince." Mothy exhaled deeply and leant beside Wolflock. "I'm just glad for the ship to be restored to its usual, happy, harmony."

"It's only logic, Mothy. Simple yet beautiful logic. It should also please Grogen that we found the plate thief. I do have to ask something of you, though."

"What's that?"

"Please don't call me 'your majesty' or 'my prince' anymore. Wolflock is fine."

Mothy chuckled and looked at Wolflock with a half-cocked smile.

"Sure thing, *Lockie.*"

Book 2

The Case of Mothy

CHAPTER 1

Write Answers, Wrong Questions

Wolflock leaned on the smooth grey taffrail, scoffing and rapping his long fingers irritably as the breeze fluttered the letter clenched in his left fist. He'd thought it was an acceptable time to write to his little sister, Myna, detailing the events of the last week but he wasn't yet satisfied with the letter's contents. It had already been a dismally long seven days on the Silver Ice Hair and, so far, he had minimal time to himself to do anything of true enjoyment. Apparently, when aboard the vessel, the captain required all the company to take part in activities. These included all manner of foolish social events through the day like ball games, novel and history readings, evening dances and deck picnic lunches. Initially, the promise of seeing the ships' specimens in varying dynamics gave Wolflock a newfound excitement, but it only took an evening for him to realise the crew and company were primarily average in all areas of life. The blanket of frustrating boredom shrouded him once more.

"I should never have looked for that snuffle..." he bemoaned as he watched waves crash on the grassy banks in the ship's wake. *I could have continued to sneak out with Mothy's assistance and be free of these tiresome bonding activities...*

The edges of the dark blue river became increasingly mottled with autumn leaves, redressing the earth in her new gown as the sleepy pink twilight lingered longer during each dawn and dusk. The very earth itself seemed to struggle to wake in the morning and crave an early night's rest as the days grew colder.

A flash of movement caught his eye to the left, and he stood bolt upright, trying to glimpse the source. *Nothing... must have been another fish...*

He had been waiting to see the maramuti creatures Grogen had spoken about, which remained the only reason he was outside and risking another social ambush calling him to some other mundane engagement. He wouldn't have minded Mothy's company, as he got along with the lad very well, but there was no one else on the ship was of any interest to him. Mothy wasn't educated in many academic schools of thought, but he had a refreshing perspective on life. He'd travelled a bit while he was younger, and he told Wolflock he'd gotten a short education in mining, blacksmithing, carpentering, farming and tailoring. Everything practical and trade worthy had at least been touched upon in his life, giving him a curious insight that Wolflock had fed off for many hours of entertainment. There was no reason to distrust his word as he didn't appear to try to show off his skills, but rather just seemed excited to share his knowledge. He had unknowingly presented himself as so naïve and genuine that Wolflock had no desire to deny his company. It also helped that Mothy hung off every word Wolflock spoke, which was a pleasant change from the constant dismissal he received from the older passengers.

He sighed and watched as pale-barked maple trees trickled their leaves into the river that lashed against their roots. Behind the dining hall was one of the few places people didn't venture too often. Wolflock had felt that he could get some peace and quiet, but even in the serenity of the autumnal landscape before him he couldn't silence the chatter in his mind.

Had his father recovered from the political drama in Plugh? What was Myna studying today? Was she tutoring Ginia? Had they done what he said and fed the good apples to the horses? How was Brennan, his horse?

He wanted a way to contact home besides the letter in his hand that he wouldn't be able to post until they reached Irid in over a month. His heavy chest heaved a sigh as he realised that he didn't want to be alone, but he didn't want to be with any of the passengers. He wanted to be with his family. He just didn't want to be in Plugh.

Wolflock continued to wallow miserably as he gazed out, catching another tiny splash from an excited fish catching insects. The scent of bread being baked in the oven from the kitchen just behind him began to creep over his shoulder. He found it difficult to pretend he was in solitude as the song hummed by the days chef in the kitchen came through clearly. Judging by the gruffness and the style of song it was Goden's job today. The longer he waited for the song to pass and his silence to resume, the more the chatter of the passengers grew as they settled on their picnic blankets for a sunny deck lunch. The sound wafted around the dining hall on the wind like an irritating bug that aimed directly for his ears.

His sulking didn't last for much longer though as Mothy bounced around the corner with a smile as bright as the midday sun.

"Merry meet, Lockie," he chimed.

To his knowledge, Wolflock had never had a pet name before and he wasn't yet sure if he enjoyed being called 'Lockie' or not. He hadn't protested because, although it was new to him to not be addressed as "Mr Felen" or "Master Felen", it wasn't entirely unpleasant. He also felt the need to have someone to talk to on the ship who at least appreciated his conversation. On top of all his other reasons for liking Mothy, he liked that he admired Wolflock for his most prized quality. His wit.

"Merry meet, Mothy," he sighed and folded his letter away in his trouser pocket.

"Are you still being grumpy?" The blond boy smirked and mirrored his position against the railing.

"I'm sure I don't know what you mean," Wolflock sniffed indignantly.

Mothy drew a long, deliberate breath in and exhaled as if he'd just smelt the best baked goods in the world.

"Isn't this incredible?" He slapped his hands on the banister. "I mean, just look at that! We're on a ship heading to another country. We get this amazing view and we get to stay with such fabulous people. We are so very lucky! We don't even have to work!"

Wolflock raised a sharp black eyebrow.

"I fail to see how a change of scenery is lucky. People worked hard to get to this point in their lives. I don't believe that luck had much to do with it."

Chuckling and shaking his head, Mothy closed his eyes and listened to the wind and water for another deep breath. "You know you have to stop being so grumpy. You're not making any friends being foul about everyone else being allowed out on deck and not just you."

"Well, I was the one who found the snuffle. I'm the one who deserved the reward. They have gotten to share it for the week and now they should descend below deck until they do something of equal use," Wolflock grumbled and crossed his arms. "The least the Captain could have done is asked if I actually wanted to share it. They were all on here for two weeks and did nothing to rectify the situation."

"You should be content that you've brought so much joy to the people here and benefitted the whole ship. Isn't that reward enough?" he asked maternally.

Wolflock felt patronised as Mothy acted as if he were teaching him how to share.

"Well, frankly no!" He raised his nose. "I thought

they would be far more interesting company but now it appears that they are just like the Plugian common folk. Now I am just hoping to get peace and quiet-"

"And find a way to get the run of the ship? All the ship for you to make you so much better than the common folk below?" Mothy snorted dryly looking through him with keener eyes than Wolflock had seen from him.

Wolflock fell silent, feeling the sting of being reprimanded. He turned away, pretending to just watch for more maramuti.

Mothy chuckled and stepped closer, bumping his elbow to Wolflock's. Wolflock refused to respond. Mothy wriggled closer and pressed his whole arm against his friend's rolled up white sleeve. Wolflock caught him in his periphery and turned his head sharply away.

Childish... he sniffed, pulling a disgusted face in order to suppress a grin.

Mothy caught it and snickered, pressing his arm even tighter, nearly pushing Wolflock along the banister.

"So... did you want to show me how amazing and brilliantly learned you are, my duke?"

Wolflock rolled his eyes so hard his whole face moved with them until they locked onto Mothy's glittering bluish grey ones. He had noticed, over the week, that Mothy's eyes changed colour slightly from day to day. Sometimes vibrant sky blue, sometimes aqua and sometimes hints of brown that glinted golden. The only people Wolflock had known to have this phenomenon where Seers, people gifted with the enhanced sixth sense of aura vision, but Mothy had laughed it off and scratched his chin thoughtfully when Wolflock questioned him about it, saying he knew nothing about it.

"I told you not to call me by those titles. If you must know, my father is a Lord. He owns a bit of land that has residents on it. That makes him a Lord. We're not related to the royal family in any clear way. I assure you."

Mothy pulled his head back as if he'd just tasted something dreadfully bitter.

"Well, I certainly won't be calling you that! Anyway, lunch is nearly ready, and I want you to show me how you do your thing."

"My thing?" Wolflock frowned as they began walking to the midship.

"Yeah, yeah! The thing you do when you look like a fortune teller but, really, you're just looking at all the bits of a person that they haven't hidden, which gives away their secrets. I want to know how you do that!"

"Well, my dear Mothy, it is simply the skills of

observation and deduction. One must glimpse the little details, know what they mean and then put all the pieces together to make a whole story."

"Sounds easy. Like a puzzle?"

"More or less." Wolflock gave a half nod.

"Well, this will be a good test of your puzzle solving skills. You can tell me about the other passengers, and I'll tell you if you're right. The only people who have been on the ship longer than me are the crew."

Wolflock found the idea intriguing and a small smile crept onto his face. He could once again impress his friend and feel proud of his honed abilities.

As they approached the mid-deck, he saw the same tartan patterned picnic blankets as the crewman, Goden, brought out platters of hard cheeses, vegetables on skewers and cliffberry marmalade sandwiches.

"I can certainly entertain the notion." He sat down across from Mothy on the same blanket as Froderyk, the rude coughing gentleman, his wife, Fuhji, and the Ulukenic woman Haatji.

"Merry meet," Mothy smiled to the group as he took a sandwich. "Wolflock is going to show us his trick. Perhaps start with... Froderyk and Fuhji."

"What? What's this now?" Froderyk's brow furrowed and his eyes shot around.

"Oh yes! A game! That will be delightful!" Fuhji giggled and laid her hand on her partner's clenched fist.

Wolflock eyed them intently, Fuhji smiling as if she was about to get her palm read and Froderyk glancing about with tight lips.

Wolflock focused and what he picked up on instinctually began to take shape. It was like looking at the pieces of a beautiful beetle for the first time with a magnifying glass. Every leg, hair, and a piece of shell glittered before him and created an image of the whole being.

Fuhji sat with a straight back, prim and proper, her hands delicately laying across whatever she touched. Her eyes had a subtle almond shape and her cheekbones were high on her smooth face. Her boyish short brown hair was showing the slightest signs of new growth and she had occasionally raised her hand to her shoulder as if to feel for something. Her left hand sported the fainter skin where a ring once wrapped around her wedding finger, but her right hand had a fine silver ring with a huge clear, twinkling gemstone in it. Her nails were painted but had grown out and the polish was very good quality judging by the lack of cracks and persistent shimmer.

Froderyk, on the other hand, hunched his shoulders forward and his skin was more weathered than

Fuhji's. He'd clearly seen a lot more sun and work than his wife. He sported a detailed silver band on his wedding finger and adorned his neck and wrists with thick gold and silver jewellery. Wolflock spied a glint of an earring under his coarse brown hair before a vein began throbbing in the sour man's temple. His mottled brown eyes, thin lips and overhanging eyebrows gave him a rather doltish appearance, even if he wore fine clothes. His shirt was currently unbuttoned, but Wolflock couldn't mistake the crisp collar and precise cut of his own tailor's family style.

"Stop looking at us!" he snapped.

Wolflock sneered.

"How am I meant to show Mothy what I do if I'm not able to do it? Anyway," he pointedly turned to his friend and waved his hand to dismiss the lesser man. "Fuhji here is one of the daughters of a noble family in Corl. I assume it is the Korsaki family who immigrated to Corl to sell grains and now control the Quarenth grain farming standards. My aunt Liona often tells us she has tea with them-"

"Are you Quathie's cousin? I used to love her embroidery. It was always the most beautiful at tea," Fuhji chimed with a glowing smile.

Wolflock stopped and blinked at the interruption.

"I don't speak much with my family in Corl."

"Oh." Fuhji leaned away and averted her gaze.

"As I was saying, Fuhji has been born amongst the circle accustomed to wealth and refined etiquette training. She was also engaged for many months, most likely to the son of another family who was believed to be of political or social advantage but with whom she had only a passing interest in, if that. Her hair has been shorn off, so she was harder to identify whilst leaving Corl, likely to have made her look like a young man or Froderyk's brother, rather than his wife.

Then there is Froderyk, who apparently came from poor breeding and earned his wealth but would never be considered by one of the better families due to their distaste in new money. His defensive and over-protective nature all come from a place of insecurity, since he knows those he covets the company and appreciation of so intensely will never accept him. Due to this, it's likely that he was raised in the worst parts of Corl, as is shown by the typical thickly set brow and more squared features of his face. He also has a conveniently nasty cough, so I wouldn't spend too much time near him for fear of catching his illness-"

"Hah!" Mothy laughed loudly, but Wolflock could see the strain on his face. "Good one, Lockie! You're such a joker. Take no notice, Froderyk."

A few people from neighbouring blankets had turned to see what the crackle of anxious energy was but turned slowly back to their food when Mothy spoke up. Fuhji began cooing affectionately to her husband, drawing the fiery redness from his face as if her words were cool water.

"Did you just dismiss me?" Wolflock asked incredulously, hurt that his friend would brush him off like that.

"Yes. Were you trying to pick a fight? Because that's how you pick a fight. When I asked you to show me how you used your smarts to figure things out, I didn't mean for you to be mean to anyone." Mothy shook his head apologetically. "Besides, if you're going to aggravate someone, you should probably not do it to someone a head and a half taller than you."

"Brains always beats brawn," Wolflock retorted.

"Not when the brain is in a pampered boy of fifteen Summers and the brawn is a man who had to fight for everything he ever got and worked three jobs."

"I'd like to see him try`

After a long pause, Mothy asked, "You don't speak to many people, do you?"

"I'm sure I don't know what you mean. You asked

me to tell you what I saw, and I told you. I did nothing wrong," he shrugged. It was of no consequence to him what Froderyk thought.

"Well... why don't you try to tell me something nice about someone else... What about Dlumi?" Mothy had caught her eye and waved.

Wolflock raised his eyebrow. He knew a few things about Dlumi already. He had walked passed her room a few days ago, noting the typical, if not old-fashioned, business trunk with bands carved with sigils of the goddess of fortune and protection wrapping around it, but it had been left open with only a few items of clothing thrown into it. The case itself was outdated. Most business people these days had more compartments for various items and a separate section for their own belongings. Dlumi frequently wore a gold-plated necklace and a copper bracelet, but both were tarnished, showing their true worth, and lighter patches of skin revealed where she had sold her other jewellery. Her skin was tanned from being in the hot sun of the South, but her broad shoulders and towering height told him she was a native of central Shiriling.

"I see nothing kind about lying for the sake of anyone's feelings. If I can see their secrets, then clearly they are not hiding them well and my evaluation does them a service so they may either come to grips with the reality of the situation or try to hide them more effectively."

Wolflock drew in a breath and began his verbal torrent.

"That being said, Dlumi is an incompetent business woman from Corsh or somewhere nearby, leaving after she fought with her family. And of course, because she comes from central Shiriling, her education has revolved around chopping trees and carving stone, which explains why her business style is antiquated and holds no relevance to how business is performed in more sophisticated areas. Her tarnished jewellery only just hides the lighter skin on which it was previously adorned, telling us that she had to sell the jewellery she wore rather than the wares she meant to sell."

Dlumi let out a choked cry and grasped her wrists, trying to hide her shame, but Wolflock ignored her.

"It's likely that she purchased these items early in her journey but was unable to identify them as being of low quality due to never having handled such things before. She began in Shellinden and was forced to move North in order to try to establish her business after her ineptitude moved her closer and closer to home. Now, with nothing left, she is returning home to beg for more money or skulk back and do whatever her family demands of her. But let's be honest, it probably a safer bet than venturing out again to try her hand at another pipe dream. If she had left with her family's blessing then she would have just been able to write them a letter and not return in person, wasting time and money."

Dlumi's grey eyes became stormy with rage and her bear-like face contorted into a snarl. Mothy's gaze darted back and forth with fear as he moved between Wolflock and the reddening Corshwoman.

"Lockie... Uh... Maybe no more?" he swallowed.

"What? You asked me!" Wolflock protested and banged his fist into the deck, making Mothy flinch. "It's my turn now. I get to pick someone. This is a grand game! A real kicker!"

Every person's eyes and ears were on Wolflock as he persisted with fervour. He would not be silenced. This would not be Plugh all over again! He would not be pushed around for the sake of others' games.

Smiling smugly his eyes focused in on the Blickland sisters.

"Ah! Look there. Ungul."

The near silent muscular woman with skin like night. She never smiled and was never away from her sister. Silver tattoos wrapped emblazoned flames around her body. Her tightly braided hair made her forehead stretch even further back, giving her a hawkish look. Her black eyes blazed around, burning anyone who appeared even slightly curious about her and her sister's presence.

"Yes, that is her. Good work. Let's get some food-"

But Wolflock couldn't care less.

"You can see by her disagreeable demeanour and taciturn attitude that she has many secrets, none of which she guards particularly well. Again, the education in the Blickland forest folk is primarily survival and not as sophisticated as Shellinmerth or Grothener. She's clearly guarding her sister from escaping again after she fell pregnant to a man who resided in Shellinden, which is where they boarded. The stretch marks on her hips and stomach say that she was pregnant to full term, as does the customary midwife bracelet on her wrist with the infant bead. But the question here is where is the man and the child? The man clearly had no intention of honouring the woman or the child, the stress of which could have caused a miscarriage or stillbirth which is why there is no man, no baby and a sister captive to her family duties. As Blickland folk seldom leave their forest, I can assume your family lives in the southern border which means the man was travelling, which then tells me that this was a sordid affair, not approved by your parents and the man believed it would be a very temporary thing. But what kind of parents don't approve of love affairs? Noble ones. Ungul and Uhnha are the children of a Blickland noble family and to prevent disgrace, Ungul as the eldest child went to drag her sister back come fire or high water! The reason I know that? Because older siblings always get that face of resentment for having to defend their impetuous youngers!"

Wolflock didn't know when he had stood up, but he found his arms outstretched, his voice growing louder and his tone becoming more commanding. He was putting on a show to shut down anyone who would tell him to be silent ever again.

Finally, he turned back to Mothy, sneering down at him. He had won. He had not been silenced, and he had shown the ship his prowess. None of them could question his intelligence. None of them could tell him he was wrong now.

Mothy looked like a ghost.

His eyes were wide, and he looked terrified. But he wasn't frightened of Wolflock. He looked past him.

Straight at Ungul.

Wolflock turned and saw Ungul rising like a dark dragon. Dlumi, too, rose like a bear, and Froderyk like a pit bull. They had their hungry, raging eyes fixed directly on him and they wanted blood.

"Ah... Lockie..." Mothy gulped and, in one smooth motion, he crouched on his toes. "Run!"

To keep reading, follow this mysterious link:

https://rhiannoneltonauthor.com/product/book-two-the-case-of-mothy/

Dirk Myna.

I habe dieser lahter findet di gut. Es hab nur par
Dinge seit von bedeutung gesehen einst di zu mich af am
serbruckt sach und I werde es hier notieren

Zuerst, I loste ein kline Geheimnis. As der Kapitans
Schnuffel habe war verschwunden. Is was ein tastiche
silberne farbe. Is scheint das der Kapitans Jamale hab ein
bedeutendes erbe von habet der helbet silberne har etlan der
silber Fluß.

Ich sagen dis ein Ihre Werbung. Saget das sich auch
de drigen zwei ein drachen. nicht anehnich zu unserem
iebel veren. Kpnigen Raein. Ich sage das ein graser
silberne drachen wer beherrscht alle rasser kunste und
prtarten drigen hir und jetzt sich kannen sicher segeln
uberall

Wahr ob nicht das bleibt abzuwarten zu es zin, aber
iz macht kumf eregante kleinikeiten. Der Schnuffel
elbet was wurze kennt es ein hausten zwi der kline Maehen
wir zauf am der sachen. Ihre menam iz Linni und Ihre iz
nihlien zu ausgehenden miteiner habet ein unheimlich rarum
berichten natur.

I was ziemlich bezauberte vom ihre. Ihre mutter
ziemliche ein drochress gehnet ihre gehen vermist

I glaube ihre mutter wurde schlafena jedenan der
diesem tagem gleiche tag, aber an dis zeit tag ihre haben
nur wurste und aufgewacht ihre chind was vermist.

Ihre suchte hoch und rief, aber ihre konnte nicht finde
ihre.
Ihre dann warden ziemlich verstert und fand mich, wer haben
fand drohen grossten von der zusammengestellt hatte. Der
spinnen netz technik I funkohiene is entwickelt werkicht gut.
Better als dine nalliger "gedanken palast". I ließ
nich fasen unberuhrt und fand ihr ein der rumf.

Der Kapitan was mechtig bittet und entfernte
auferte der Passagier beschrankung zu par ein det. war
konnte nicht hab nur ein gründe. keine gründe wahl es war

da rbqgb mbhr gollbn nqcht an dqb bbnbtqgbn alg gpbbqlgt
grom dbr gpbbqgb gaal zu ungbrbm Kabqnbn wurdb rbqgbn.

Nqchtgdbtomqnbr. Igt bn Gchnuffb gab nah bggbn mqch
bqnbn nachbr. I fragb gqch gut gq konntb vbrklbqgbn bqnbq
und uf qg qz lbhnt habbt bqn gg bqn haugbn. Gch gchbqn zu
habb bqn kogtqchb Bbrdauung bqg dbr gpatbrbn Jahrbng gor
zb qg auch bg muhgam zu rqngbn qg zu bqn gtadqum dg qg
qz qqftqgbr Wartung.

Gtbllqbr dat gor!

Eqn gbchgqlngbn vbrklbqgbn!

I mug fqndb wbg brgchroggb gbm bqn bbgchaftqgt
Jbmand hab hattb gbzogbn dbr nachbr.

Zwbqtbng. I glaubb I habb gbmacht bqn frbund
Ihr mbnam qz Mothg und Ihr qz bqnbm gbltgambr tVp von
ragamuffqn rbrl. Praktqch zu hab qbbbnbn und zqbmqlch
qffqzqbnt am macht mqch lachbn. I wqrbg bg bqttbt zu habb
Ihrm qbbbnbn fumf dbr bqnlagbn. Wbr konntb wbg unfug wqr
wqrbg rqngbn ungbrbmbq bqnzu.

I bqn nqcht zu gblangwbqlt. abbr qg auch kommtb btlan
qrgbndwann. I wqrbg aufdbm gq laufbndb. I habb allb
qz gut vom dbr angbnund bqttb macht btllan Barta
futtbrtb dbr pfbrdb dbr gut Apfblb, nqcht zur dbr
gbqubtbchtbn bqnb.
Gch gagbt bgh kannbn tbrkbbqt dbr gchbachtbn.

Dqnb brgbbbnbrt Bruthbr.

Wulflack F. Felen

About the Author

Rhiannon is the walker between worlds. One foot in Earth, the other constantly stepping into Pelaia. As if gazing into a crystal ball, she sees this other world and all that happens within it with the clarity of someone staring through a veil. It is her purpose in life to transcribe these histories, adventures and mysteries for you to enjoy.

This witchy woman was raised by a fairy who taught her that there are all kinds of magic throughout the world. She taught Rhiannon to withhold judgement because you never truly know another's story. She also taught her that everyone, no matter how flawed, has something to give.

The adventures of Rhiannon's youth lead her through trials and dangers that taught her about the darkness within the world, but it also showed her that anything could be overcome. There was always a way. Surrounded by so much apathy and hopelessness, Rhiannon made it her goal in life to show others the light and that if they could dream it they could do it.

The way she was shown this was through stories.

Stories of friendship, love, adventure, discovery, compassion, understanding, and kindness. All of these stories gave her new friends, new lessons, new life.

In the depths of her darkest place during year 11 and 12, when she felt at her loneliest, drugs surrounded her life in terrible ways, the self worth of those she loved and admired crumbled, she was relentlessly bullied and felt friendless in her most trying years, she lived in squalor due to bureaucratic errors, and yet she still had to be "perfect". She had to perfectly excel in school, she had to perfectly remain calm and gentle in the face of abusive men, she had to be a perfect role model for all those around her. That craving for perfection in order to get love nearly killed her several times. In all of this darkness with politicians sacrificing real people and real environments for imaginary money, with teachers displaying no compassion for their students, with men abusing women and children, with communities vilifying those who needed them most, with injustice reigning and all hope seemingly lost... Puinteyle was born.

All of these pains in life were fixed in Puinteyle.

All of them were able to be mended and healed because of a conscientious effort. The people of Puinteyle wanted to be better than their problems. Puinteyle was where people made an effort to love freely and always sought to help each other, animals and the environment. Harmony. True and beautiful harmony. Where the pendulum never swayed too far away from that beautiful harmonious and happy point of balance.

But like in our lives, there is always obstacles to overcome and darkness to understand. Therefore, Puinteyle would always have its own inner turmoils to learn and grow from too. Thus, the stories never truly end.

Rhiannon has always lived and breathed stories, knowing her role in life is to be this guide through a new world for others. Her dream is to support her community with her stories, as well as creating a company where other artists can come together in celebration of Pelaia and all it has to offer.

Get More of the Magic & Mystery…

subscribe.rhiannoneltonauthor.com/more

If you want more clues, more magic and more mystery, let me know by going to the Case of the Captain's Hair subscribe page.

You'll get clues, maps, sketches, behind the scenes stories, lore and much more! You'll also be the first to know when a new story is coming out so you can solve the mystery before your friends.

If you sign up with the magical link below, you'll also get a free downloadable map to follow Wolflock's journey to Mystentine University.

subscribe.rhiannoneltonauthor.com/more

Thank you for being part of the magic and supporting an independently published Australian author! Australia's independent authors need the support of their local community to continue to produce the books we all love.

If you enjoyed this book, please leave a positive review online (where you purchased the book or on Goodreads), recommend this book to your friends or family, or purchase another copy to gift to a loved one.

Stay tuned for the next mystery in the series:

THE WOLFLOCK CASES

BOOK 2

THE CASE OF MOTHY

www.rhiannoneltonauthor.com

 RhiDElton

 RhiannonEltonAuthor

 RhiDElton

 rhiannoneltonauthor

 Rhiannon D. Elton

 RhiDElton

THE WOLFLOCK CASES